POSITIVELY DIFFERENT

Positively Different

KENDRA GALE

For the members of the Miniature Horsemanship Study
Group and Book Club - a more encouraging group of
Miniature Horse lovers doesn't exist anywhere!

Chapter 1

Emma closed her fingers on the reins and gave a strong squeeze with her inside leg as she turned the big horse towards the final line of jumps. Thor gathered himself beneath her; she could feel his tension as he gnashed the bit in his teeth and fought the tie down, and she braced herself for his anticipated run out.

"Not today, big boy," she said, keeping her eyes focused straight ahead, past the neatly braided mane and through his ears towards the jump, using all her strength to block his attempted bolt past the jump and force him over instead.

He cleared the first jump of the final line and she held her breath. *Only two more to go and we've won!* She urged him forward with a tap of her crop on his shoulder as he thundered towards the in and out, then leaned back in an effort to shorten his strides. Her hands ached with the effort as she tried to balance nearly fifteen hundred pounds of unpredictable animal, but it was all going to be worth it when he won this class – everything they'd worked for, all her dreams coming true.

She heard her coach call from the sidelines, "Shorten him up!" and she pulled harder just as he hit the final stride before launching into the air, and then they were over and Thor snorted, a big loud dragon noise, as she felt him rebalancing for the second jump and gave him his head just as he changed his mind and hit the brakes, swerving hard to avoid the jump.

Emma grabbed for his reins to catch herself, but it was too late and she tipped, pulling the big horse further off balance until they both went down. Emma saw the jump standard coming closer and then everything went dark.

"Emma! Can you hear me?"

Emma groaned and turned her head away from the insistent voice of her coach.

"Emma!" Ainsley was still shouting at her, so Emma made an effort to open her eyes, and then realized that her shoulder hurt. A lot.

"Ow," she said out loud.

"She's awake!" Now it was her mom's voice she heard and that made her pay more attention.

"Mom?"

"It's okay, Em, the ambulance is on it's way, they're going to take good care of you, just lay still." Her mom spoke in a soothing tone, but Emma could hear the worry beneath it. She opened her eyes to see her mom's familiar face smiling down at her, and Ainsley on her other side, her eyes wider than usual and focused one hundred percent, which was weird as she usually was watching four riders and her phone at the same time.

Emma tried to sit up, but they stopped her. "I think I'm okay," she tried to insist, "I just hurt my arm."

"Wait until you get checked out, Em, you took a terrible fall."

"What about Thor?" She moved her head as much as she could with someone's restraining hands on either side of her neck, but couldn't see the big horse anywhere. "Is he okay? Where is he?"

"Maria took him back to the barn," Ainsley said, her voice deliberately soothing, "he'll be fine, just worry about you right now."

Emma heard the ambulance siren approaching in the distance and tried to take inventory of the damage. Her shoulder hurt a lot; she must've hit the jump standard, or the ground, or maybe Thor's foot. She wiggled her fingers tentatively and gasped – nope, bad idea, now her whole arm was shooting with pain. People talked at and around her, but she tuned them out and tried to wiggle her toes instead. Yep, those worked, and without any alarming consequences like the finger wiggles. She squinted into the sun – everything was a little bit blurry and there was a pounding in her head. She moved her eyes to follow the movement as paramedics took the place of Mom and Ainsley and her head spun like she'd just got off the teacup ride at the fair. She squeezed her eyes closed and concentrated on answering the paramedic's questions.

Yes, she knew her name, where she was, what happened. Yes, she was in pain, her shoulder hurt, and her arm. No, she couldn't wiggle her fingers, well, okay she could, but it really hurt. They shone a bright light in her eyes, which made her squeeze them shut again, and then they were strapping her to a backboard and loading her into the ambulance and then they were on the way to the hospital and the lights and siren and vibration of the wheels over the pavement made her head swim and her stomach swoop and then the paramedic spoke to her reassuringly and put a needle in her arm and she drifted off.

Chapter 2

Emma opened her eyes slowly, blinking at the sunlight through the familiar daisy curtains in her bedroom. Usually they made her smile, but today she scowled. Morning again, but what was the point in getting out of bed. She couldn't go to school because she was supposed to be resting her brain after the concussion. She couldn't go to the barn until her shoulder healed, and since they still weren't sure if she was going to need yet another surgery who knew when that would be. And she wasn't allowed her phone or even a book, as that sort of concentrating was also hard on her healing brain. At least the headaches were getting better, but still, what was she supposed to do all day?

She tried to roll over, but her shoulder and arm in it's sling and carefully propped on pillows wouldn't let her, so she used her good arm to pull the blanket over her face, blocking out all that nasty cheerful sunlight.

"Good morning!" Her mom sounded deliberately cheerful and a little tentative which made Emma realize how grumpy she'd been since the accident. She sighed and pulled the blanket back off of her face.

"Morning."

Mom helped her sit up. The huge, padded sling really helped stabilize the shoulder and made it so much easier than it had been a week or two ago, but she still appreciated the help. "Thank you," she said, and she really meant it.

She took the pain and anti-inflammatory meds that her Mom handed her and swallowed them with some water.

"I have good news!" Mom said, "It's been two weeks, that means that you get to go outside for a walk today, and you can even watch some TV!"

"Can I have my phone?" Emma asked eagerly.

Mom made a sympathetic face. "I'm sorry, no – the doctor says that it's still too soon for that. Your brain needs a bit more time." She kissed Emma's forehead. "I know it's not ideal, Em, soon though! But a walk will be nice, won't it? Some proper fresh air will be just what you need! And I've already got the remote by the recliner and Netflix fired up. Breakfast is on the table, and there's lots of snacks. Granny will be by at lunchtime." She smoothed Emma's hair back from her face and cupped her chin. "You'll be okay?"

Emma smiled for her, trying to ease the worried lines between her eyes. "I'll be fine, Mom, thank you. It will be fun to go outside for a bit."

"Good." She kissed her forehead again and stood up. "Don't overdo it, just to the crabapple tree and back today maybe?"

"Sounds great Mom, have a good day at work."
***

Emma jumped when she heard the door open, then winced. Her shoulder wasn't THAT well supported for a sudden movement. She rubbed the incision across the top of her arm tentatively and called, "Granny?"

"Have you been sleeping in front of the TV all day?" Granny marched in and turned off the TV. "Well, I guess that's resting your brain, but it's time to get up and at 'em!" She set a paper takeout bag on the table next to Emma. "I brought you McNuggets." She kissed Emma's forehead just like her mom always did. "How are you feeling?"

"Okay. Tired. Bored."

Granny checked her watch. "I've got twenty minutes, lovey, before my next showing." Granny smoothed her tidy pantsuit. "Let me tell you about this couple I showed a house to this morning.

With a tummy full of fast food and laughing at Granny's crazy realtor stories, Emma did feel more energized than she had in days and considered the walk her mom had suggested. She carefully got to her feet and went to the window to look out.

It was a beautiful day, with the fall colours starting to show, and nothing but sunshine and blue skies, but still Emma looked back at the comfy recliner longingly. It was only the idea of having to tell her mom that she hadn't gone out that made her head towards the front door.

After staring at her paddock boots for a moment, remembering the last time she'd worn them, she slid into her crocs. There's only so much someone with only one useful arm can do, shoe-wise. She grabbed her hoodie, put it on awkwardly with only one arm in a sleeve, and headed out into the sunshine.

The sun made her head ache, so she ducked back into the house, plopped a ball cap on her head and a pair of her mom's ugly wrap around sunglasses, and tentatively stepped back out. Much better, the brain approved.

It wasn't far to the crabapple tree at the bottom of the yard, but Emma took it slow and careful. She watched her feet closely ... last night she'd tripped on the edge of the bathmat and jarred her shoulder and she was in no hurry to repeat the experience. One foot after another, slow and steady she found her way down to the tree at the edge of the property and plunked herself onto the bench in the shade.

She was out of breath.

That was frustrating.

Two weeks ago she'd been riding the biggest, strongest horse in the barn over a jump course at the biggest show of the year, and now she got winded walking down the back yard.

She shouldn't have thought about Thor. She really missed him, and all the other horses at the barn. She didn't have a horse of her own, but it was like Thor was hers, she'd spent so much time with him, and she really missed him. She'd heard, finally, even though everyone had tried to keep it from her as long as they could, that he had been hurt in their fall, and was on stall rest for a suspensory injury.

He was so beautiful, and now he was lame, and it was all her fault.

She ran through the accident again in her mind. There had to be something she could've done differently, something that would've kept him safe. Kept her safe. If she'd just been stronger, or quicker. If she'd done something different when he'd tried to run out, maybe, or warmed him up longer.

Emma closed her eyes. She could see Ainsley saying it wasn't her fault, that Thor was just a wingnut sometimes, there was no way of knowing that he would duck out, and he was so big and strong Ainsley figured even she wouldn't have been able to stop him. He would heal, she'd been assured, and even if he wasn't sound enough to return to the jumper ring, he could do hunter, or maybe even dressage – he sure had the size and movement to be competitive. Maybe that would be a nice change for her too, leaving the big jumps behind. Emma pictured herself cantering towards a fence again in the future and her muscles got so tense that her shoulder started to ache.

"Breathe," she said out loud to herself, and it helped. She took another deep breath and started to relax. She watched the sunlight dapple through the leaves onto her feet. The grass was still green, with the yellow leaves starting to fall, and the colours were beautiful. Emma took one more deliberate breath and tried to just enjoy the moment instead of thinking about how much things sucked right now.

She reached for her phone thinking she'd take a picture of the leaves, and then remembered she wasn't supposed to have screen time. She sighed. Maybe she should look at Instagram ... at least she got herself stopped before she actually got her hand in her pocket this time.

Maybe her mom was right, and she was addicted to her phone.

Whatever, big deal.

She was so tired anyway.

Emma stared up the slope towards the house, thinking longingly of her bed, or at least the recliner in front of the tv. The bench wasn't super comfy, but the sun was warm and she leaned back, pulled her hat down low and closed her eyes.

A piercing whinny made her jump hard enough that she hurt her shoulder and gasped, shoving her hat up and grasping her aching shoulder with her good hand as she jumped to her feet and spun around, wondering if she'd drifted off and dreamed it.

Their yard was big, but it wasn't big enough to house a horse, and all the ones nearby were the same. She'd never heard a horse in their neighbourhood before, but she was sure that's what she'd heard.

She turned in a circle, trying to decide which was a likely direction for the whinny to have come from, and nothing looked likely. She leaned on the back of the bench, still gingerly rubbing her shoulder.

Maybe she did dream it.

A sound of crunching leaves made her turn, and a tiny horse wandered into view, grazing on the lawn as it walked.

It was small, and dainty, with a bright copper and white patterned coat, a long silver mane, a tail that brushed the grass as it moved, and bright blue eyes. It wore a turquoise halter, and dragged a matching lead rope.

It seemed like something out of a dream ... until it stepped on the lead rope, jerked its head against the pull and backed up hard, nearly falling as it slipped on the grass.

"Oh!" Emma said, and the tiny horse spooked at her, snorting in alarm. She froze along with the pony, hoping it wouldn't run off entirely, gone as quickly as it appeared.

Bouncing sideways, the tiny horse eyed her suspiciously for a few moments through those brilliant blue eyes, and then cautiously dropped his head and cropped another mouthful of grass.

Emma took a cautious step forward, then another, speaking quietly while the pony continued to graze, but was definitely keeping an eye on her.

"It's okay little man, no need to run off, I know all about horses, if I can just get that leadrope ..." as she spoke she lunged, her good arm reaching for the end of the leadrope that trailed a distance beside the little horse.

It worked! She got a good grip on it, and just had time to feel a flush of success before her quarry spooked hard at her sudden movement, hit the halter with a crash, and nearly yanked her good shoulder out of the socket, leaving her with nothing but rope burn as he galloped around a small group of trees and out of sight, the lead rope trailing through the air like a ribbon.

Emma sank to the ground.

That was a bad idea. She didn't think she'd done any damage to her injured shoulder, but it sure hadn't been good for it, and the usual dull ache had intensified into a much sharper pain. Her head too wasn't impressed with her decision making skills, throbbing as her poor brain had been sloshed around once again. She stared at the angry looking areas of shiny red rope burn stinging like crazy on her formerly "good" uninjured hand and seriously considered going straight home and back to bed.

But then she looked in the direction that the tiny horse had disappeared. What if he got onto a road, or tangled in a fence? She couldn't just leave him without trying to get him somewhere safe.

Slowly, she got to her feet and began trudging after him, thinking about a plan – she definitely wasn't going to be able to try the old "grab and hold on" idea again, not in her condition.

She imagined what her mom would've said – heck, what her mom WOULD say when she saw the rope burn. She was always telling Emma that she needed to stop thinking she was invincible.

For once, Emma thought, tallying up all the sore spots, Mom might have a point. Time to be smart, instead of using brute strength.

Holy smokes that tiny pony was strong! She'd once caught a runaway thoroughbred in a similar manner – of course, she wasn't already recovering from a serious injury then, but still, this one sure was able to give a similar yank considering it was a fraction of the size.

Emma walked on, quickening her pace, her aches and pains fading to the background as she focused on the problem in front of her. If she managed to catch up to him again – and that was seeming like a bigger IF all the time – then she would have to try to corner him, she decided, and make sure she didn't give him a chance to spook and bolt again, because there was definitely no way she could hold him.

In fact, the idea kind of scared her. That was new – she didn't remember ever feeling scared of anything to do with a horse before, and this was a teeny tiny horse. But she really didn't want anything to do with the idea of being on the other end of that lead rope again.

She was walking along a green space, behind a series of back yards and saw a movement up ahead, catching site of her small quarry as he ducked through an open gate into an enclosed yard. Yes! That was perfect! She tried to run to get to the gate and close it, but her shoulder and her head both told her an emphatic NO to that idea, so she just lengthened her stride and crossed her fingers that he wouldn't pop back out again before she got there.

She watched as he milled around, tromping through flower beds that luckily were mostly done blooming for the year as Emma suspected the home owner probably wouldn't like a pony in their petunias. Just as he decided it wasn't that interesting after all and made a move towards the open gate, Emma was able to make it the last few steps and swung it shut in his face. Once again, the pony snorted and backed up, his head high (well, relatively, he was really small, like the smallest horse Emma had ever seen) and staring at her suspiciously from underneath a silvery white forelock that hung nearly to the end of his nose. His bright blue eyes (Emma had also never seen a horse with blue eyes in real life before) regarded her suspiciously for a moment before a noise behind him made him spin away and trot off into the corner of the yard.

Emma also jumped at the slamming door.

"Is that your pony?" A lady who was much shorter than Emma, but with much taller hair came storming out of the house, her arms swinging at her sides as she stomped towards the gate and spooked the animal in question so it ran through the flower bed again, throwing stems and clods of dirt into the air behind it. "My bulbs, it's going to ruin my bulbs!" She turned on Emma, glaring up at her. "Get it out of my yard!"

Emma took a step back, tempted to flee for home, but she couldn't see leaving a poor innocent animal, even one responsible for her rope burned hand, in the clutches of this Karen.

"He isn't mine," she said, surprised by how squeaky her voice sounded. She steeled herself against the fury of the bulb lady. "I was just trying to catch him so he didn't get into any trouble."

"Well, you failed at that, didn't you." The Karen looked on in dismay as the pony, calmer now, nosed through an ornamental hedge along the other side of the yard. "Help me chase him out of here."

"No!" Emma's voice was loud in alarm. "This might be the only chance to catch him, he's contained in there!"

"Well, catch it then." The Karen crossed her arms. "Be quick about it, before it does any more damage."

Not at all confident, Emma slipped through the gate, double checking it was latched securely behind her. She surveyed the situation – there was a garden shed at one side of the yard, near the corner, so there was a reasonably narrow gap between the shed and the fence, with a dead end created by the corner of the chain link fence that surrounded the yard.

"If we can get him in that corner, I think I can get a hold of the lead." Emma pointed towards the corner.

The Karen didn't move, staring at Emma blankly.

"If you stand there," Emma pointed again at a spot midway across the yard, "to cut him off I think I can head him into the corner."

The Karen sighed and rolled her eyes. "This isn't my problem, you know."

Emma shrugged. "I can do it myself, but it will probably take me a few tries, especially with this." Emma lifted her hoodie so the lady could see her bulky supportive sling. "And a lot more horse tracks around your yard."

The creator of said horse tracks, who'd been standing on the opposite side of the yard regarding them warily, cocked his tail and let loose a steaming pile of road apples squarely on the neat stone pathway. It looked to Emma that he'd had quite a bit more green grass than his system was used to on his adventure – instead of neat dry balls, the manure hit the stone with a wet splat.

"Ugh," The Karen made a disgusted face, but it seemed to spur her into action and she moved to the place that Emma had indicated.

Emma went wide around the pony, who turned to look at her but didn't bolt away until she got to the far side of him and waved her good arm enthusiastically to head him back towards the garden shed. He leapt into action, his feet skittering on the stone walk, spraying his recently deposited manure an impressive distance.

When he neared the spot where the Karen stood, she shrieked and ran away, but that scared him enough that he turned anyway and headed into the corner, right where Emma wanted him. Her good hand on her bad shoulder to add some extra support, Emma winced against the pain as she ran to block the gap.

She got there just as he wheeled to come back out past the corner of the shed and shouted and swung her arm to send him back in. He sat back on his haunches, his long silvery mane flying in a cloud around him as he spun to avoid her, turned and gathered himself in one smooth movement, and sailed over the three foot tall chain link fence.

Emma stood, mouth open, watching the perfect jumping form of the smallest horse she'd ever seen as he effortlessly cleared a fence that was taller than he was and gave a series of joyful bucks as he thundered away into the distance.

Chapter 3

Emma didn't even hear what the Karen was grumbling about as she ushered her out of the yard and latched the gate securely behind her, and she only wandered a short distance after the pony before she stopped.

The weight of the day's events suddenly settled onto her with a bone deep exhaustion. After two weeks in bed and two surgeries she wasn't quite up to an afternoon of hiking around after a delinquent equine, and her shoulder and her head throbbed.

But the pony ...

She stared in the direction that he'd gone for a moment, then shook her head. She wasn't doing a bit of good on her own. She needed rest, and reinforcements.

She was further from home than she thought and by the time Emma stumbled up to the front door all she really wanted was back in the comfy recliner in front of the TV, but the phone was ringing as she punched the code to unlock the door and she rushed inside to pick it up.

"Em?" Her mother's voice on the other end of the phone sounded beyond worried, edging into frantic, "are you all right? I've been calling for over an hour! I've already had Granny leave a meeting early to come check on you and I was about to follow her home!"

"I'm fine, I'm sorry!" Emma felt awful for scaring her. "I didn't mean to be gone so long." Quickly she relayed the unusual adventure she'd been on.

Her mother gasped at the part where she'd tried to grab the lead and Emma had to reassure her that she didn't need to go get her shoulder checked out, and then she laughed incredulously at the report of the tiny horse who could jump a fence that was taller than he was.

"You rest, Em, Granny will be there soon, and I'll get on the neighbourhood Facebook group and let them know he's been spotted. I think that's all we can do for now though, you need to take care of yourself. Take your meds! Rest!"

Emma did as she was told, and was just swallowing the painkillers and anti-inflammatories with an entire glass of cold water when Granny rushed in calling, "Emma, are you here?" with an urgency that told her that she hadn't yet got the text from her mom letting her know all was well.

"Yes!" Emma called, hurrying to let Granny know she was okay, and grateful for the cautious (in allowance for her shoulder) hug and familiar kiss on her forehead. Emma gratefully sank into the comfortable recliner at last and was just settling an ice pack on her shoulder when Granny's phone binged and she pulled it out and read it, her eyes opening wide.

"I told you to go for a walk, not on a wild horse chase!" Granny said sternly, but her eyes twinkled. "Tell me everything."

Emma got her love of horses from her Granny, who had never been able to indulge in her own fascination and enjoyed Emma's equestrian pursuits vicariously. It took no time at all to get her just as invested in the plight of the runaway as Emma had been. Granny checked the local Facebook group, and read Emma the post her mom had made.

"My daughter tried unsuccessfully to catch a miniature pony at the edge of the park near Cove Street at around 2 this afternoon. Pinto, white mane and tail, blue eyes, dragging a turquoise lead rope. Headed east."

There was a stream of comments underneath from others who had seen it too, and one that had to be from the Karen: "That little beast DESTROYED and CONTAMINATED my yard – if you own it please contact me immediately to make reparations!!!!"

There was nothing from anyone who was missing him, but that didn't seem surprising with a comment like Karen's on there – Emma didn't think she'd want to admit to owning him either in that situation.

Granny looked at her watch. "I've got an hour til my next meeting ... want to go have a drive around and see if we can spot him?"

Settled in the passenger seat of Granny's SUV was a much more comfortable way to hunt for a tiny horse than trudging along with an aching shoulder. Emma turned on the heated seats.

Based on the posts on the Facebook group, when they'd gone east past Crazy Karen's house they turned north up another side road. Emma watched carefully while Granny drove slowly, each peering down the spaces between houses, and then they did another loop through the alley, still without any luck.

Once Emma spotted a flash of golden reddish fur and jumped hard enough to make her shoulder hurt, but it was just a big golden retriever out for a walk.

There was a small park with a playground at the end of the next street, and they went past extra slowly. Emma opened her window as she tried to make sure she looked past all the swing sets and play structures, but still, there was nothing. Some kids playing, but no sign of a rogue equine, of any size.

"Well," Granny said, sounding disappointed, "I think we're not going to find him, lovey."

"One more road?" Emma looked at her hopefully.

"One more road." Granny nodded and turned on her signal light.

Emma leaned forward eagerly as the last road came into view and then sat up so straight she bumped her head on the roof.

There, in the middle of the road coming right towards them was the same tiny horse, mane and tail flying as he charged along, but he was hindered by a tall and strong looking teenage boy, who had caught hold of the leadrope and was scrambling to keep his feet under him while leaning backward for all he was worth.

The car coming towards him made the pony slow and change direction, and the boy was able to gain some traction and turn him, getting a hold of the leadrope further up and bringing them both to a stop.

As soon as the car stopped Emma leaped out and hurried over as fast as she dared without spooking the horse again.

"You caught him!" She grinned at the tall teenager holding the lead and eyeing his capture suspiciously. Then she looked closer. "You're Jake, right? You go to Central High?"

"You grabbed the lead on THAT!" Granny said behind her sounding incredulous. "It's a wonder he didn't yank your other arm out of it's socket!"

Jake nodded. "He's strong for a shrimp." His eyes flickered to Emma, and she could tell he didn't recognize her. But she didn't really expect him to, she was two grades below him, older kids never did pay any attention to the younger grades.

"Do you know who he belongs to? Is he yours?" Emma was surprised to see that now he was solidly under control the pony seemed to have no inclination to resume his wild ways, instead standing quietly, not even looking at her as she approached.

"Nah, not mine, but I know where he belongs." Jake turned and began to walk away and the horse followed without protest, plodding along behind him. He couldn't be more different than the plunging beast they'd seen when they came around the corner, or the one that had leapt the fence so majestically and bucked joyfully off into the distance.

Emma followed along. "But, he's so good now!" She was puzzled by his behaviour. She was sure he would've been wild and difficult to lead, but here he was, head down, stepping along without putting a foot out of place.

"Yeah, that's how he is, I guess. Once he knows you've got him he's no trouble."

Emma continued to follow, though Jake didn't seem inclined to want to stick around and visit. "Where does he live?"

"Next subdivision over. My neighbours place." He glanced over at Emma, and seemingly reading in her bright expression that she wasn't going to go away without the whole story, sighed and stopped. "My neighbour bought him at an auction for her kids. They keep trying to play with him, but he just puts his head down and runs off on them. Goes through fences too, they had to lock him in a shed to keep him home." He started walking again, the little horse following docilely at his side. "This is the last straw, she says, wants me to take him back to the auction mart tonight, pass him off to some other poor sucker who thinks he's cute."

Emma looked wide eyed at her Granny, who was right behind her listening. Granny read the silent plea in her eyes perfectly.

"No need for that, young man, what did you say your name was?" Granny's businesslike tone made him start and Emma wondered if he hadn't noticed her before or if her boss lady voice scared him.

"Um, it's Jake, ma'am."

"Jake," she handed him her business card. "Please take him home and get him securely in his shed so he cannot escape again. Give this card to his owner and ask her to call me. I have a meeting that I need to get to, but I will give her whatever she paid for him. He's my granddaughter's problem now." She winked at Emma.

"I don't know if that's a good idea ma'am," Jake looked at Emma and her bulky sling skeptically. "This pony is a demon, it's all I can do to hang onto him."

Granny answered before Emma could, putting a hand on her good shoulder to keep her from saying anything. "She'll have to be careful then, won't she. What's the address?" He rattled it off and Granny told him that she'd expect the call from the owner of the pony and would have transport organized for later this evening, or tomorrow morning at the latest. Then she looked at her watch. "Come on, lovey, or I'm going to be late, and I still have to break it to your mother that I've bought you a tiny demon." She grinned roguishly and swept Emma back to the car.

Once inside she immediately dialed the phone, holding up a finger to stem Emma's rush of thank yous and excited questions, and Emma thought she was calling her mom until Ainsley's voice answered over the speakerphone in the SUV.

"Ainsley, it's Rosemarie Jacobs, Emma's granny."

"Oh hi! Is Emma doing okay?"

Granny looked at Emma.

"I'm here Ainsley, I'm okay, guess what?!"

Granny broke in again.

"So, Emma and I have done something a bit crazy, Ainsley, and we're hoping you can help us make it work."

"Oh?"

"Do you have a space at the stable for a very wild and escape artist miniature pony?"

"Um .... What?"

Granny grinned at Emma. "Emma went for her first walk post surgery today, and somehow managed to find a rogue tiny pony who is in a bad situation for him, being kept in a shed and headed for an auction because he keeps dragging kids around and getting away."

Ainsley laughed. "Of course she did! Only you could find a horse on your first walk post surgery Em!"

Emma grinned. "Can he have a stall?"

"I'm sorry Em, we're full up, and sounds like it wouldn't be safe to keep him in any of our outside pens — we don't need him getting in with the bigs and getting hurt. But I think I have a better idea, closer to home for you even — let me make a call and I'll let you know!"

"That would be great Ainsley, thanks," Granny said, "one more thing, are you free tonight to haul him?"

"Oh yes!" Ainsley sounded delighted, "I want in on this crazy adventure, just text me when and where!"

Chapter 4

"You did WHAT?!"

It was possible that Emma's Mom wasn't quite as delighted with this turn of events as Ainsley had been.

"It'll be fine, Soph." Granny ruffled her hair affectionately while Mom stared at her. "You'd have done the same thing if you'd been there, it'll all work out, you'll see – I'm late, must go!" Granny strode out of the door, leaving Mom shaking her head, but she had a smile on her face.

She went to the freezer and grabbed an ice pack, handed it to Emma and pointed at the recliner. "You, rest," she said, "and tell me the whole story."

Emma had just gotten to the part where Granny had called Ainsley when the house phone rang and Mom said, "Speak of the devil," when she looked at the caller ID and answered it, "Hi Ainsley – I hear they've roped you into this crazy plan too!"

Emma could hear Ainsley laugh over the phone, but the rest of the conversation sounded more serious, with her mom just saying, "oh" and "I see" and nothing of Ainsley's part of the conversation audible to her.

"Okay, thanks for the update, Ainsley, we'll see you later for pony shenanigans!"

This time Emma could hear Ainsley's response: "I can't wait!"

Mom hung up the phone, slapped her hands down on her knees and stood up briskly. "Well, if we have a busy evening of miniature pony fetching tonight we better get some food into us!"

She made for the kitchen but Emma stopped her with a question.

"What was Ainsley talking about?"

Mom stopped, and Emma could see her sigh before she turned back, kissed her on the forehead and sat down nearby on the edge of the couch.

"Ainsley said that the vet came to see Thor again today."

"Is he okay?" Emma sat forward anxiously, and her mom leapt up and gently laid her back as she answered, readjusting the ice pack on her shoulder.

"He's fine," she spoke soothingly, "they're just concerned that today's ultrasound didn't show much healing in the tendon, so they're planning another procedure, some high tech thing that involves spinning his own blood for stem cells, to help promote healing."

Emma's eyes filled with tears. Her own injury was far easier to handle than his was. "It's my fault. And he's not getting better."

Her mom squeezed her hand reassuringly. "He WILL get better Em, just like you, he just needs some more repairs from the doctors."

Emma shook her head and finally said out loud the words that had been spinning in her mind ever since she heard that Thor had also been injured in the fall. "If I was a better rider it wouldn't have happened. If I'd done it differently Thor wouldn't have been hurt."

Her mom hugged her cautiously, squeezing her tight while avoiding the injured shoulder. "Don't you think that way! Thor could've gotten hurt out in the field, and even if it was your fault – which I'm sure it wasn't – did you do the very best that you knew how?"

Emma sniffed against her shoulder. "Yes."

"Then that is all that anyone can ever do." She rocked her gently back and forth. "All you can do now is keep learning and keep growing and maybe you'll be able to learn something new that will make sure it never happens again." She drew back and looked Emma seriously in the eyes. "And maybe not too. Horses are big and strong and also fragile and things don't always go according to plan."

Emma nodded miserably. She wasn't sure she believed that it wasn't her fault, but she felt better having gotten it off her chest.

"Besides," her mom smiled at her, "the vet is the one in charge of worrying about Thor at the moment, we have more pressing matters to worry about!" She checked her watch. "We have less than an hour til Granny's meeting is over and she'll be ready to start going full speed into Operation Wild Pony! Let's get some food and get organized!"

***

It was getting dark when they turned down the last road towards the address Granny had gotten from the owner of the wayward small equine.

"What did she say when she called you, Granny?" Emma asked, wondering if she was a nice lady or not.

"She said she got my card from Jake and if I wanted the pony – she used a few other four letter words to describe him – that I should just come get him, so I told her we'd be there with a trailer this evening and not to let him get away again before we got there."

"And Ainsley?"

"She's going to meet us there, and she's lined up a great place for him to live – a farm that used to raise Miniature Horses, but now they just a have a few elderly retirees. He'll have friends like him, and fences made to keep small equines in – and it's close enough that you can even walk there, if you're motivated!"

"Once you've healed a bit more." Mom put in. "Not yet, you're supposed to be resting – I have a feeling you're going to be paying for today's excitement tomorrow."

Emma waved her good hand dismissively and leaned forward eagerly from the back seat as she spotted Ainsley's trailer was up ahead of them with it's turning light on.

Emma recognized the smaller trailer, the one she used to take horses to and from the vet and other local smaller trips, instead of the huge gooseneck they took to horseshows and clinics away from their home base of Stone Ridge Stables.

Good thing too, Emma thought as they followed her into a tiny yard. Ainsley was very practiced at maneuvering the truck and trailer into tight spaces but she thought the big trailer literally wouldn't have fit in what was basically a back yard, not a farm yard at all. A series of small wooden buildings – Granny called them granaries – stood along one side of the yard.

A tired looking lady with frizzy dark hair came out with a fussy baby in her arms and a crowd of small children trailing out behind and around her. Emma thought there were four, but then spotted another peeking out the door.

Granny went to talk to her, and Ainsley walked over to the SUV, a big grin on her face.

"Tell me about this horse, Em!" She said cheerfully. "What colour is he?"

"I'm not sure," Emma said, knowing that Ainsley, always the horsemanship instructor, would want his "proper" colour. "He's a sort of coppery reddish brown, with pinto markings, a silvery mane and tail, and two blue eyes."

Ainsley's own blue eyes opened wide in surprise. "TWO blue eyes! Neat! Can't wait to see him!"

Granny gestured towards one of the little wooden buildings, and they walked towards her as the frizzy haired lady herded the kids back into the house.

"She doesn't want the kids anywhere near that …" she paused, "pony again, but asked that Jake fellow to come help us, says he should be here soon."

The building she indicated looked just like all the others. It didn't have any windows or anything, and didn't really look like a good spot for a horse to live, even a tiny one, but it was sturdy and there was a big carabiner snap securing the door, so that was good, all things considered.

Ainsley tried to peek through the crack, and a piercing whinny came from within making her jump, and then laugh. "Hi little man!" she called cheerfully, "can't wait to meet you!" She looked around quickly. "Why don't I back the trailer right over here? Then we just have to get him out and right back in again."

"Good idea." A grim sounding voice came from the shadows next to the building and made them jump just before Jake popped out into view. He nodded a greeting.

It took Ainsley no time at all to back the trailer up until there was just room to open the swinging door, making one nice solid barrier. With the door to the shed open the other way, they'd only have a small gap they could fill with humans. Really, the only choice he'd have would be the trailer. Jake nodded again, which Emma took to be an enthusiastic approval of the plan.

Ainsley took charge, but deferred final plans to Jake. "You know him better than us, what's the best way to get a hold of him?"

"I'll just do it." Jake unsnapped the door latch and slipped inside, saying, "hold the door til I say so," as he disappeared inside and Ainsley and Mom rushed to do so, looking at each other with eyebrows raised while muffled bangs and crashes came from inside.

"You two stand in the gap," Ainsley directed Granny and Emma into position, "I've got this door, you go too." Emma's

Mom joined them standing shoulder to shoulder. Ainsley nodded in satisfaction.

"Coming out!" Jakes voice was a bit muffled by the door and Ainsley swung the door wide open, holding it tight as part of the barrier to keep their new addition contained.

Jake had the turquoise lead wrapped incorrectly but securely around his hand, but the tiny horse was in his "well behaved" mode, walking out sedately and not paying a bit of attention to the anxious group assembled. Emma saw Ainsley's eyebrows raise in surprise but before she could say anything Jake stepped into the trailer and urged the horse to follow and he went from obedient to feral in the blink of an eye. He plunged backward, and Jake barely managed to get an arm out to brace against the side of the trailer door to prevent being pulled right out. Then the horse reared, his mouth open in a silent scream as his forefeet pawed the air and Emma drew back in spite of herself.

"Walk up on him." Ainsley's voice was calm, the result of directing a thousand dramatic horse situations. "Surround him and walk up on him." Following her instructions, the four of them made a little semicircle around him. She stomped her feet a little and the rest followed suit. It took a moment or two, but eyes rolling, their new acquisition finally took a flying leap into the trailer, and Emma wasn't sure, but she thought he might've come down on Jake's toe.

Ainsley quickly swung the trailer door closed, and without the light from inside they were now standing in darkness.

"You want him tied?" Jake's voice came from inside.

"Yes please!" Ainsley said quickly, and a moment later Jake slipped out. Granny thanked him and offered some money for his time but he shrugged and mumbled that it wasn't any trouble and headed off into the darkness, seeming eager to disappear as quickly as he'd come.

He was limping.

Chapter 5

"I'm going to have to do some research," Ainsley said as they drove away with their new charge, "I'm with you Em, I don't know what that colour is called! One of the dilutes that we don't usually see in warmbloods and thoroughbreds, whatever it is it's beautiful! And those blue eyes!"

"He is beautiful." Emma liked riding in the truck with Ainsley. It was never dull as Ainsley kept up a steady chatter of horse talk, tonight focused on the tiny equine in the trailer. She glanced out the side mirror at Granny's headlights and wondered what the conversation was in the other vehicle between Granny and Mom. She'd seen her Mom give quite a significant look of concern to Granny when the trailer door had closed behind the rearing and plunging horse. Tiny though he was, Emma knew her mom was worried about her safety.

Like she was reading her mind, Ainsley said, "You're going to have to be careful with him Em, especially at first because you are still healing." She took one hand off the wheel and pointed at Emma, her eyes still on the road. "Strictly hands off for now, no grabbing that lead or halter, nothing but hanging out and maybe trying to pet him. Over the fence."

Emma nodded. Carefully. The truth was that a very full afternoon of excitement had taken its toll, and she was very willing to listen to the advice of caution right now. She was exhausted and her head ached and her shoulder ached, but it didn't dull her excitement about the new horse.

"I'll be happy just sitting by his fence," she said, "mostly I'm just really happy he's not still locked in a shed with no windows, or running around on roads trying to get hit by cars, or attacked by wild Karens."

"What?!" Ainsley burst out laughing. "Wild Karens? Oh wait, tell me that story later, we're here!" She turned on her signal light.

Emma leaned forward eagerly as they pulled into a farmyard with a cute red barn and lots of nice mesh wire fences that looked both secure enough and tall enough to hold her new horse.

Emma felt a little thrill. *HER new horse!* She'd never had a horse of her own before, and she wasn't sure she could've been any more excited if it had been one of the fancy show jumpers she'd always wanted. HER OWN HORSE, and he was beautiful.

The truck came to a stop and a quick walking lady appeared in the headlights, a brightly patterned scarf wrapped over her neatly curled grey hair as she waved enthusiastically at the truck. Ainsley leapt out of the truck and ran to embrace her, and Emma got out more slowly – she really was getting sore – and arrived just in time to see the lady pull out of the hug and hold Ainsley by the shoulders like she just wanted to look at her.

"It's so good to see you, Sissy, even better than hearing your voice on the phone this afternoon!"

Ainsley hugged her again. "I'm sorry it's been so long since I visited, I'll come back soon, I promise." She turned with a grin to Emma.

"Emma, this is Ruby Waters." Ainsley linked arms with the older woman companionably. "I was younger than you when I first started hanging around Ruby's yard and pestering her for time with her Miniature Horses."

Emma extended her hand in greeting. "I'm Emma, thank you for letting this horse stay here with you!"

Ruby shook her hand warmly as they were joined by Granny and Mom. "Oh well, I never could say no to this one!" She jerked a thumb in Ainsley's direction with a twinkle in her eye.

"Thank goodness you didn't!" Ainsley said, "Or who knows what I'd be doing now!"

Ruby laughed. "Oh, horse girls always find their way to horses, you might've had a different path but you'd have gotten there in the end."

Once the introductions were made, Ruby got businesslike. "Let's get the poor little guy off the trailer, sounds like after what he's been through he'd like to get out and stretch his legs, come see what I've set up for him."

The other four trailed after her like ducklings, and though Emma would've called her an "old lady" if she'd been asked, Ruby was fast and Emma found herself struggling to keep up.

"I can't let him too close to my old folks," Ruby was saying, "until he's been quarantined, since he's come from an auction not long ago. The rest of my herd are now well over 20, at their age they can't handle any viruses or anything, so your wee man is going to have to quarantine for a while. He'll be able to see them though, and suspect he'll be much happier for it, and less likely to want to roam."

She opened a gate and they all walked into the pen and looked around. It was a large paddock, and Emma could see a cozy looking shelter bedded with straw, and near the gate they'd come through was a nice clean pail of water and a fat flake of nice looking green hay. Ruby saw her looking and grinned. "I know it's probably too much for him, but I wanted him to feel welcome!" She turned and put a hand on the fence, shoulder height for her. "It's also my tallest fence, I used to use this for my stallion, and Sissy mentioned that he'd been an escape artist."

"That's good!" Emma said, "I saw him jump a 3 foot tall chain link like it wasn't even there!"

"Oh, they're good jumpers, these little guys," Ruby said, "But this should hold him, and if it doesn't I think he'd probably just head over to visit the pensioners instead of exploring." She turned and sped back out of the gate, tossing over her shoulder, "Well, shall we get him settled? Poor thing stuck in that trailer while we stand here chatting."

"I'll back the trailer over here closer." Ainsley jogged off to the truck and trailer and Emma took the chance to ask the question she'd been itching to ever since they'd arrived.

"Why do you call Ainsley, Sissy?"

Ruby laughed again, her eyes crinkling in a way that showed many decades of laughter. "Oh when she started showing up here, my boys were grown, just ready to go off on their own, and she was here so much they started joking it was like they suddenly had a little sister, and started calling her "Sissy" – she hated it at first, but it grew on all of us." Her smile was wide. "My Tom, he still asks when he calls if I've heard from Sissy and if she's still jumping the moon on those big horses of hers."

'Sissy' (it made Emma giggle to think of her as that) backed the trailer expertly to right near the gate, which Ruby held wide, and Granny, Mom and Emma all assumed their positions, ready to block any escape routes while Ainsley first peeked into the trailer door cautiously, "Oh, good boy, still tied up and not in a bit of trouble!"

She popped inside letting the trailer gate swing shut behind her and there wasn't even any banging or crashing before she called, "Okay, here we come!" and pushed the gate open wide.

As soon as she stepped down the little horse shot forward, but Ainsley was ready for him, with a firm grip on the lead near the halter and braced against him to bring him up short. She grinned, "He IS strong! And his technique – he's definitely done that before and got away!"

Just like a switch, once his usual charge didn't work, he stood at her side, without even looking around him, and walked quietly into the pen when she moved forward, and Ruby closed and latched the gate behind them.

Emma leaned on the fence to watch.

"The last owners were letting him drag the lead to be able to catch him, but I'm guessing that's not the plan at your place Ruby?" Ainsley winked.

"No way." Ruby was emphatic. "I put some panels in the corner there," she pointed and Emma saw a couple solid looking metal panels making a mini pen in the corner of the large one. "If we need to catch him we can run him in there and put him behind one. Won't be any trouble, and he won't hang himself. No horse on my place wearing a halter around unattended, let alone a nylon one like that. Break his pretty little neck."

Ainsley grinned. "I knew you'd say that." She reached for the buckle on his halter, and he twitched his head away from her, in the biggest reaction he'd given since the first charge out of the trailer, but he still didn't move his feet. "It's okay big boy," Ainsley murmured, "Did you think I wanted to touch your ear?" She went more slowly and was able to unbuckle the halter, slide it off, and give his neck a little scratch. "Oh, those halter marks!" She tried to touch his nose where the obvious line of the halter ruffled his hair and made his nose look dented, but as soon as she reached for his face he backed away. "All right, you explore your new house then!" Ainsley climbed over the gate and joined the rest leaning on the fence to watch him.

He seemed to come alive as soon as he was free and all the humans were on the other side of the fence. He threw his head up, blue eyes reflecting the yard light, and silvery mane flowing as he trotted animatedly in a large circle, then began pawing and circling looking for a good spot to roll. He rolled in the dry dirt ground, going over and over, and they played the game of saying he was worth another $100 for every time he went over, and he was pretty expensive by the time he stood, shook and leapt into the air in a huge buck.

"Oh, that does your heart good, doesn't it?" Granny put a hand on Emma's uninjured shoulder. "I think we've done a good thing for him, I'm not sure he's been able to do normal horse things like that in a while, other than on his unauthorized outings."

"Ruby will know the answer to our question, Em!" Ainsley said, then quickly asked it, "What colour IS he?"

"He's silver bay," said Ruby, "that's a bay horse, with the silver gene, which dilutes black pigment, which is why his mane and tail are more diluted than his body. And a beautiful shade of it too, so golden with that nearly white mane and tail, he's lovely! And those eyes!"

"Is silver bay a common colour in Miniature Horses?" Emma asked, enjoying learning something new.

"Fairly common yes, but he is a striking shade, not as common. I've got a silver bay here, you can meet her in the daylight tomorrow, and she's much darker than he is, her shade is much more common. What's his name?"

"I ... don't know!" Emma said, at a loss. How had she never thought about his name all this time!

"Hang on," Granny strode off towards her car, "The lady gave me an envelope with a bill of sale and stuff, maybe his name is on there."

They gathered around to see as she pulled out the contents of the envelope.

On the front was a bill of sale, where he was listed quite anonymously as "brown and white mini pony".

"Maybe he hasn't got a name, Em, you'll have to think of one." Mom said.

Granny flipped up the first page and Ruby said, "Wait!" when she saw the page underneath. "That's a copy of his registration papers! He's not a random "mini pony" he's a registered animal!"

"Oh!" Emma bounced a little in excitement, "What's his name?"

Granny squinted at the paper in her hand. "Midnite Ranch Lightning's Snookums."

Granny and Mom looked as confused as Emma felt. "That's his *name?!*" Emma said incredulously.

Ruby and Ainsley laughed. "Miniature Horses always have bonkers registered names." Ainsley explained. "The 'Midnight Ranch' part is the farm name of his breeder-" she peered at the paper "- whoa, he's come all the way across the country! And then Lightning will be his sire's name," again she referred to the paper, poking it with her finger "yep here it is Midnite Ranch Mighty Lightning, and then his name is Snookums."

"Snookums?" Emma wrinkled her nose and Ainsley laughed again.

"You don't have to call him that, you can call him whatever you want. Lots of horses don't go by their registered names, just like our horses at the barn usually have a barn name and a show name. But if you show him at a sanctioned registry show, he will have to be Midnite Ranch Lightnings Snookums then."

"But you don't have to decide tonight." Emma's mom was looking at her with concern. "I think it's time you were home to bed young lady, your day has been approximately forty-seven times busier than it should've been for your recovery."

Emma looked reluctantly at her new horse, now nibbling happily at his hay.

"I'll check on him before I go to bed," Ruby said reassuringly, "and I'll give your mom a call first thing to let you know how he did overnight."

"And I'm free midmorning tomorrow," Granny said, checking her calendar on her phone, "so I'll run you back to see him then!"

"Oh, and if you're up to it," Ainsley said, "I'll pick you up after lunch so you can come visit your *other* horse baby Thor!"

"I'd like that!" Emma let her mom start to lead her towards Granny's SUV, then stopped and turned back to Ruby. "Thank you," she said. "So much."

Ruby winked at her. "We are going to have fun with him young lady! I will see you tomorrow and introduce you to the rest of the geriatrics!" She nodded her head towards the little red barn.

Bundled into the SUV, Emma was already nodding off by the time they made the short drive home.

Chapter 6

Emma was riding Thor, but something was wrong. Instead of the tightly coiled spring feeling of his muscles ready to move at her slightest direction – or even without any direction at all – he felt dull and listless beneath her. She looked down and realize he was limping badly, with a gaping wound on his leg. Blood dripped from it, leaving red hoof prints behind him.

How did that happen? Ainsley said he had hurt his ligament, not that he had a gash like that. She jumped down and looked around for help.

But she wasn't at the stable, she was at the miniature horse farm, and there was her new little horse, looking excited to see Thor. His silvery mane floating around him he gathered himself to jump a fence, but it wasn't the same tall sturdy woven wire fence she remembered, instead it was barbed wire, and the post was broken so the wires were loose.

"NO!" Emma shouted as her beautiful new horse jumped, and his legs tangled in the wire. He thrashed on the ground, embedding the barbs into his legs, blood running down his white socks.

"NOOOOOOOOOOOOOOOOOOOOOOOOOOOOOOOOOOOOOO."

"Emma!"

Emma awoke, a scream still in her throat and tears streaming as she fought free of the sheets. She sobbed as her mom's arms went around her and held her tight, smoothing her hair back from her face.

"It's okay Em, it's just a dream, nothing but a dream, it's all right."

Emma worked to get her breath back. "Did she call? Did Ruby call yet?"

Her mom rocked her gently in her hug, like she was still a baby. "Yes, I was just coming to wake you and tell you, she said he is happy as a clam in his pen, and was excited to see the other horses when she turned them out, but not TOO excited just interested and showing off a bit. She says he's going to fit in beautifully!" She looked Emma in the eye. "Was your bad dream about him?"

Emma nodded, fresh tears coming to her eyes as she thought of her dream again. "He tried to jump a barbed wire fence, he got all tangled up and he was bleeding, and Thor was bleeding too, and I couldn't get any help."

"Shhhh, the little man is safe, Thor is safe, and you're going to see them both today so you can verify that with your own eyes, I promise."

Emma took a deep breath and tried to forget the dream. It was just a dream. It wasn't real. They were safe. Well, Thor was hurt, but he wasn't bleeding and hopefully he would heal. Hopefully ...

Her mom looked at her with concern in her eyes. "How is your shoulder? Is the pain what's giving you nightmares?"

Emma hadn't really thought about it, but the shoulder was aching. "Maybe. I think it will feel okay after my meds though."

"I'll get them!" Her mom jumped to her feet. "You lay down for a minute!"

Emma did as she was told and tried to calm her still racing heart with deep breaths that still came out a little shaky. "They're fine," she whispered to herself, but the reassurances felt hollow. The little horse was fine, but Thor wasn't, not really.

The little horse. He really needed a name. They really couldn't continue calling him a zillion variations of "the small horse" much longer.

Snookums.

That WAS his name, officially, so Emma thought it was only fair to give it proper consideration.

She closed her eyes and pictured him. He was little enough to be a Snookums, but far too handsome in her opinion to pull off something so cutesy. She wished she had a photo to look at – she did some quick math, it was still five more days before the doctor said she could have her phone back, as soon as she did it would be full of photos of her little blue eyed, silver haired whirlwind.

Whirlwind.

Emma grinned to herself. It suited him, but it was a bit girly. Plus, he didn't really whirl, he just put his head down and went. Something else along those lines though?

Storm.

That was better, even went with Lightning, which was part of his name too. It still seemed kind of like a girl's name though, for some reason she couldn't identify.

Lightning.

It was part of his name after all, only fair to consider it. But didn't Ainsley and Ruby say it was his father's name? Maybe not then. He deserved his very own name, not his dad's, specially when he probably didn't even know his dad. Emma giggled at that thought.

Okay not Lightning but ....

Thunder!

Hmm ... Thunder.

She closed her eyes and pictured him again. Her favourite moment to remember, when he'd amazed her by jumping the fence that was as tall as he was and then tossed that beautiful mane and thundered off into the distance.

Thundered off into the distance.

Thunder!

She grinned and opened her eyes to see her mom looking down at her in surprise, carrying a glass of water in one hand, and a pill bottle in the other.

"Well, you improved while I walked to the kitchen and back!" She set the class down and helped Emma sit up.

"I think I might've figured out what his name is!"

"Snookums?"

Emma laughed. "I did try it out, but he's really not a Snookums, he's too serious for that."

Mom nodded and laughed too. "He is definitely too serious for that. So? Don't keep me in suspense, what are we calling him?"

"Well, I want to see what Granny thinks, and Ainsley and Ruby too, but what do you think of Thunder?" Emma watched closely to see her reaction.

"Yes!" Mom's face lit up. "Thunder suits him, the way he thundered out of that trailer!"

Emma took her pills and headed to the kitchen for her breakfast, looking forward to her day for the first time since the morning of her accident and took a deep breath. A shadow of her nightmare still followed her, but she pushed it away.

It was going to be a good day.

***

"I think it's perfect!" Granny said when Emma told her the name she had thought of. "So much better than Snookums."

Emma leaned forward as they got closer to the farm. Granny turned on the signal light just as Emma spotted a sign she hadn't noticed the night before.

Cool Waters Farm Miniature Horses

"How did we never see this place before Granny? It's so close to our house!"

"I'm not sure, lovey, just not quite on the beaten track I guess." Granny drove right over to park near the big paddock where Thunder (name pending) was munching on his hay, looking like a civilized equine.

And, Emma thought, *he is still where he belongs and has no legs caught in wire or bleeding. It was just a dream."*

"Good morning, Thunder!" Emma leaned on the gate and held her good hand out towards him. He did lift his head from the hay, blinked his blue eyes at her, and then continued to watch as he dropped his muzzle back to his breakfast.

"I think he likes it!" Granny said, a smile in her voice.

"Good morning!"

Emma jumped as Ruby's voice came from close behind her.

Ruby laughed, "Sorry didn't mean to startle you, I'm told I'm sneaky like that. Did I hear you call him Thunder? That's perfect!"

"You like it? I wasn't sure, but then I remembered the way he thundered off after he jumped the fence and thought maybe it would suit him."

"It definitely suits him, and it's nice to have something to call him." Ruby joined Emma leaning on the fence. "He is a beautiful boy, I look forward to seeing you two become friends."

"Friends," Emma first smiled at the idea, and then frowned, "How do I do that?"

Ruby smiled at her. "First step is just what you're doing now. Spend time near him, asking nothing of him. Talk to him. Let him know you're not a threat to him, that you're not just going to try to drag him around like everyone he's ever met in his poor little life has done. A Miniature Horse is small, people are always manhandling them, and while most of them are so good natured they just put up with it, some of them, like our new friend Thunder here, take offence and fight back. First step to being friends is to not ask anything of him at all."

Emma watched Thunder chew his hay for a few minutes, thinking about that idea. She hadn't ever thought about the idea of "making friends" with a horse before. Her goals had always been to make them do something, but Thunder wasn't a normal horse with a normal history with humans. She nodded seriously. "I can do that. I'll come every day."

Ruby's smile widened. "Would you like to meet the rest of the four legged crew?"

"Yes!" said Emma at the same time as Granny said, "I would!" and they followed her across the yard.

With eyes only for Thunder when they'd arrived, Emma hadn't even noticed that the paddock around the little red barn was now full of tiny equines, most of them Thunder's size or a little bit taller.

"How many do you have?" Emma was delighted.

"We're down to eight now," Ruby said, and Emma thought there was a bit of sadness in her voice.

"Down to eight?" Granny said, a question in her voice.

"Yes," Ruby said, "Back when your Ainsley first started coming here more than fifteen years ago," she paused, "wait, might be 20 years nearly now, we had around 30."

"Thirty!" Chorused Emma and Granny.

"Some moved on to new homes, but most of them have moved on to the hereafter," there was definitely sadness in Ruby's voice now. "Those dear old friends are all that's left, and they're all senior citizens, just like me. But we sure enjoy each other's company, and I'm lucky every day I still have them to look after."

"How old are they?" Emma looked around at the adorable faces, some of whom had grey shaded faces as a result of their age.

"My oldest right now is Snickers," Ruby pointed at a black one with the longest fur that Emma had ever seen on a horse, along with a nearly solid grey face, "he's 31."

Emma and Granny were suitably impressed and talked about how good he looked, and that they never would have guessed.

"And my youngest," Ruby turned to indicate a long legged looking chestnut and white pinto, "is Moonbeam, she's the baby at 21 years young."

"If I remember the paperwork properly," Granny said, "Thunder is just 5 years old!"

"Now he's the baby around here, for sure," said Ruby.

They went in through the barn to go into the pasture with the horses, and there were adorable small wooden stalls down each side of the barn, every one of them with a beautiful painted name plate. Emma read the names as she passed: Moonbeam, Dinah, Richard, Popcorn, Glitter, Snickers, Sunshine, Jimmy. Every stall had fresh shavings, ready for bed time. In a row along the rafters an impressive collection of somewhat dusty ribbons hung, of every size and colour. Emma felt like it was a magical place, full of memories, and then she saw the outside wall of the tack room. It was absolutely covered with the painted name signs, each with the same beautifully made depiction of each horse's face, and decorated with flowers, or stars, or leaves around the edges. Emma just stopped and stared and Granny and Ruby were already sliding the door at the end of the aisle open when they realized that they'd lost her and turned back.

"Are these the ones you've lost?" Emma asked softly.

"Yes," Ruby smiled fondly, "all my old friends, still here in the barn in some small way."

"Did you make the name signs?"

"Most of them, yes! But a few Sissy helped me with – lots of those little daisies around the edges are her work!" Ruby pointed one out in particular.

"They're beautiful." Emma remembered what Ruby had said last night about how important it was to become Thunder's friend before asking anything else of him, and then of all the friends Ruby'd had, and lost.

"My friend Thunder." Emma thought to herself, and then followed them out the door.

They spent an enjoyable half an hour out with the tiny herd, hearing stories about them from Ruby and petting their thick, soft coats, and watching them interact with each other. Sunshine and Moonbeam were mother and daughter, and best friends, and Emma watched them scratch each other's withers contentedly. Snickers was cranky with the others, pinning his ears and shaking his head.

"He's jealous," Ruby scolded him playfully, then hugged his little grey head, "he thinks no one but him should get any of my attention ever."

Richard was a champion in a halter class, where he was judged on his beauty and conformation, and his regal bearing even in his old age made you believe it, while Jimmy was a champion in harness, and once when Snickers chased him off Emma got a glimpse of the floating movement that had made him a favourite of the judges.

"That one is a silver bay?" Emma asked, "Like Thunder?"

"That's right!" Ruby walked over and moved the long fore-lock to the side so they could see her big dark eyes. "This is Dinah, and she's a much darker shade than Thunder is." Her body was a chocolatey brown compared to Thunder's more golden tones, and her mane and tail were nearly as dark, but with more grey and silvery tones than her body hair.

Finally, there was Popcorn and Glitter, both of them white with light coloured spots over their whole bodies. "I used to drive the appaloosa girls as a pair," Ruby said, "they were quite the talented driving team once upon a time, some of the very first Miniature Horses in this area to enter the sport of com-bined driving." She patted the matched pair as they lined up on either side of her for their turn for her attention. "Still do hook them up from time to time, on a beautiful day, or a special occasion! The girls still love it!"

Emma watched how Ruby walked among her horses, talking of them with pride and fondness, and contrasted it with the busy stable where she usually interacted with horses, where everyone was always working on a new skill or training for an upcoming competition. It felt so peaceful here, which was weird, because Emma would've said that the stable was a happy place. It was a place she was happy, wasn't she? Well, nervous, sometimes, or worried because she wouldn't be strong enough or good enough to get Thor over a jump. She wondered if she'd be scared to get on him again when they both had healed up and tried to picture it, tacking him up and leading him to the mounting block, then putting her foot in the stirrup and swinging onto his back. That wasn't so bad, maybe she wouldn't be scared. But what about a jump. That's when she felt the butterflies in her stomach. Okay maybe she would be scared. A bit. At first.

"Emma?" Granny's voice interrupted her thoughts, "You okay? Are you tired?"

Emma smiled, "No I'm fine, just thinking about stuff." Speaking of jumping ... "Ruby, do any of these horses like to jump?"

"Oh yes! Dinah is my best jumper, she loves it, though I don't ask her to jump very high these days, now she's almost 25 years old, but she still loves a few jumps now and again. Soon as you're up to running with her you can take her over a few, good practice for you for when your boy is ready to learn jumping with a bit more structure instead of freelance." She winked at Emma.

"So you run with them to get them to jump? Do you have to jump too?" Emma frowned. She was pretty sure it would take her quite a while to heal enough to jump the jumps alongside Dinah.

"Not usually,' Ruby chuckled, "no, we just go alongside the jump, and the horse goes over."

They said goodbye to the horses, and Emma felt like she wasn't the only one who was reluctant to leave the paddock of sweet little faces. Even Granny waited to give Popcorn one last pat before she slipped through the door and back into the barn. Ruby popped into the tack room for a moment on the way through and came out with a folding chair and a small pail. She set the chair up at the fence of Thunder's paddock, on a nice flat bit of ground right close to where he munched his hay and invited Emma to sit.

"You're healing, and you need to be resting, and I can't think of a better place to rest than right here watching that pretty pony eat. And here," she gestured to the pail she'd set on the ground, "there's a few horse treats you can tempt him with. Don't expect him to eat them out of your hand right at first necessarily, but you can toss them his way from time to time, so he starts to think that good things come from you."

Emma sat in the chair and grinned up at Ruby. "Thank you!" Then another thought occurred to her. "Are you allowed to call Miniature Horses "ponies"? I saw a TikTok once where a girl was saying they're NOT PONIES." She waved her good arm around in imitation of the excitable person she'd seen in the short clip.

Ruby laughed. "I've heard that as many times as the tired old joke asking if I left them in the dryer too long and they shrunk! But I don't think they care what they're called. By the broadest definition, they're under 14.2 hands, so they are ponies. And their DNA traces straight to the Shetland ponies of the British Isles. But for me, I just use 'pony' as a term of endearment."

"Oh yes!" Emma had a sudden flashback. "Ainsley calls Thor a pretty pony sometimes, when he's all braided up for a show, and he's the biggest horse in the barn!"

"See," Ruby said, "a pony can mean lots of things, but you can call Thunder here whatever you'd like him to be." She winked and turned to Granny, "Would you like a cup of tea? I have an album of photos I think Emma would like to see, but we might as well have a cup and let her spend a little one on one time with her boy before we bring it out to her."

"That sound okay, lovey?" Granny checked in with Emma, but her feet were already edging towards the house.

"Sounds perfect!" Emma hardly noticed as they walked away and disappeared into the front door. She leaned her head against the post and just watched Thunder chew for a while.

"Thunder," she said, with a bit of singsong in her voice, and while he didn't lift his head, his blue eyes did seem to focus on her. "Good boy," she said, "what a handsome good boy. I'm Emma, and I just want to be your friend." He stopped chewing for a second, as though he was listening to her, then sighed and took another mouthful of hay. "I get it," she said, "you don't really have a lot of reason to trust a human, but look at me," she gestured to her sling, "I couldn't drag you around if I wanted to right now, so all we can do is get to know each other." She realized she was chattering away to a horse and glanced over her shoulder. There was no one here, but she did wonder what the girls at school, who already thought she was a 'crazy horse girl' would say if they could hear her. She reached down and rattled the pail of treats instead to see what Thunder thought of that. He threw his head up, but his eyes and nostrils were wide, more like he thought it was a scary noise than that he thought 'yum cookies' so Emma didn't move it again, and instead sat very still and quiet until he put his head down and tentatively started eating hay again.

The last clinic she'd ridden in, when Thor had spooked at one corner of the arena, the clinician had told her to ride him deeper in the corner, to use her inside spur and the crop to not let him duck out. She said that a strong rider would force him to see there was nothing scary in the corner.

There was nothing scary about a rattling pail, either, but it didn't seem like the way to be his friend would be to make him listen to it more. Maybe it was different for big horses, but Emma couldn't think why. She leaned her face against the post again and frowned in thought. Maybe because they were so big and you could get hurt when they spooked? But Emma had done everything she could to make Thor go over the jump, and she'd still gotten hurt a lot. And she remembered Jake, limping away into the darkness after Thunder had stomped on his foot in the trailer. Thunder had been scared then, too, and Jake had gotten hurt, even though Thunder was tiny for a horse.

She was scared too. Emma suddenly remembered her nightmare, and how scared she was when Thor and Thunder were both bleeding and she didn't know how to help them. And how when her mom had come in, she hadn't ignored her fears, even though it was just a dream, and made her get over it and get up and get ready for the day. She'd held her, and reassured her, and given her a chance to feel better, to get over the fear.

Horses weren't humans, but fear was fear.

It was a lot to think about.

Chapter 7

Emma reached into the pail and took one treat out, holding it with just two fingers to avoid angering her rope burns, and careful to not make too much of the rattling noise that Thunder didn't like. He stopped chewing to watch her, but didn't raise his head, so she was pretty sure she hadn't scared him again.

"It's okay Thunder," she kept her voice low and calm, "it's just a cookie, it's yummy!" Emma remembered what Ruby had said about throwing them to him, and lobbed the treat gently so it landed near the hay pile.

Thunder snorted and jerked his head up, then reached his neck out, nose towards the treat but keeping his feet as far away from it as possible. Emma giggled.

"That's a lot of drama over one little treat," she said, "go on, you can do it! Just take a tiny step!"

Thunder sniffed suspiciously for a while, and then all of a sudden he seemed to decide it was safe, and he relaxed, stepped forward, and picked up the treat in his teeth. It clearly wasn't a flavour he'd tried before, as he nodded his head and chewed in an exaggerated fashion, then curled his lip.

Emma giggled helplessly watching him, which didn't seem to bother him at all. "Do you like it? Or hate it?" she asked him, and picked up another. This time the small rattle of the pail made his ears prick in her direction, but with less of the wide eyed alarm than before. "Does that mean you want another?"

Emma lobbed his in his direction, but with her enthusiasm moved her arm too quickly for him and he spooked and galloped a few strides away. "Oh!" Emma put her hand over her mouth. "I'm sorry, didn't mean to scare you." He watched her from what he clearly considered a safe distance, but he didn't seem to have seen the new treat, so Emma threw another, aiming for the first and moving as slowly as possible, and then removing her arm from his space and sitting still.

He watched her long enough that she thought he wasn't going to go get the treats after all, and then he blinked, dropped his head, walked over and ate the treats, one after the other, with only a minimal amount of dramatic chewing this time.

"You DO like them after all!" Emma said, and tossed another, a bit closer to her this time, and Thunder didn't hesitate, walking right over to eat it. She tried it again, and he walked another two steps closer willingly.

Ruby had said not to expect him to eat them from her hand, but he was close enough now, chewing happily on his treat, that Emma couldn't resist trying it. She extended her arm as far as she could, palm flat the treat in the center.

Thunder rocked back at first, but then stretched his nose towards her, and Emma felt a thrill and had to work to stay perfectly still. It took a long time, but slowly, slowly, he took another step forward, and she felt first his warm breath, and then, for the briefest moment, his whiskers against her fingers, but that feeling seemed to be too much for him and he backed up fast, snorting like a dragon.

Emma was disappointed, but she was trying to be his friend, and she let that guide her response. "That was a good try, Thunder! What a brave boy!" She tossed the treat in front of his left front hoof (she was getting better at this!) and he ate it without hesitation.

"That was amazing!" Granny's voice came from behind her, making Emma jump, but Thunder just kept chewing on his treat, licking his lips like he was enjoying every crumb. "He very nearly took it from your hand!"

Ruby was beside her, smiling broadly with a large book in her arms, and on top of it a small container and a can of root beer. "You'll be friends in no time at this rate!"

"I brought you a snack and a drink, if you'd like," Ruby indicated the container and Emma reached for it eagerly to find a square of iced brownie.

"Oh, thank you!" Suddenly she was starving. She reached for the can. Also thirsty. She took a big bite of the brownie, enjoying the flavours, and then giggled. "I think I'm enjoying this as much as Thunder did HIS treats!"

Ruby opened the album. "I thought you might like to see your instructor Ainsley when she was your age."

The photo on the page made Emma squeak with delight. A very young Ainsley looked out at her with neat pigtails, wearing a bright pink shirt with sparkly designs all over the sleeve and shoulders, and a black cowboy hat. She posed with a shiny black Miniature Horse, looking more like a tiny version of Thor than any of the fluffy horses they'd met this morning. The horse wore a neck sash ribbon with more ribbons clipped to the neck sash, and three trophies stood on the ground in front of them. "Wow! What horse is that! What did they win!"

"That's Snickers!" Ruby said, and Emma looked up in surprise. "I know, looks a bit different these days doesn't he? They'd won the Gelding Championship, the Youth High Point, and ..." she peered more closely at the photo, "I think the Jumping Championship?"

She turned the page, and showed a photo of Snickers sailing over a jump, ears up and knees level, showing perfect form while Ainsley was in midair too, running alongside with no feet on the ground, grinning at the camera, pigtails bouncing.

"Ainsley's first jumping horse! We should have a copy of that photo in the tack room at the stable!" Emma was delighted.

"I thought you might enjoy these," Ruby turned the pages, and Emma devoured the photos of Ainsley and Ruby and the beautiful Miniature Horses, all shined up for show and looking every bit as much the fancy show horses as Thor when he got all dolled up for a competition.

"I wonder if Thunder would be as beautiful as these horses if he was groomed for show."

"Oh, I know he would," Ruby said, "trust me, after all these years I have x-ray vision through all the floof – wait'll he sheds in the spring, he's going to be gorgeous." She looked over at Thunder and said as though in apology, "Of course, you're already gorgeous."

Emma was pleased to see she was in good company chattering away to him like he understood her. Who cares what the girls in school would've thought, they weren't here, and they didn't have a beautiful Miniature Horse of their very own either, did they?

Granny looked at her watch and said, "Sorry lovey, time to get you home, I've got a meeting, and we've got to get you fed and ready before Ainsley comes to fetch you."

Emma got to her feet and impulsively hugged Ruby goodbye. "Thank you so much," she said, "for looking after Thunder, and for the brownie, and the photos, and the treats!" Ruby gave her a warm, gentle hug, then Emma went to fold the chair and take it back to the tack room.

"No, no, leave that there, then it'll be ready for your next visit." Ruby smiled warmly, "Come visit with the big man anytime!"

When they got into the car, Emma looked over at Granny impishly and asked, "McNuggets?"

"You read my mind."

***

After a drive thru, and reminders from Granny (before she left) and Mom (on the phone) to take her lunch time meds,

Emma was feeling a little tired as she sat on the front step to wait for Ainsley to pick her up.

Ainsley was often later than she thought she'd be, because she was always going a zillion directions at once, so Emma leaned comfortably against the railing, wrapped in her warm jacket and barn scarf, to wait.

She hadn't been back to the stable since the accident, during their big annual show, in front of everyone, and she was a little bit nervous about it. It was nice she had this chance to go midday with Ainsley, instead of after school like usual when all the girls she usually rode with were there.

Not that they would say anything mean. They were her friends ... mostly. But she would have to hear about the rest of the competition after she'd been taken to the hospital, and she would have to recount her surgeries, and the ambulance ride and stuff for them, and they'd ask her how long until she could ride again, and to be honest Emma herself hadn't been quite ready to ask the doctor that question yet. Obviously not until she got out of the sling, at least, and they weren't even sure yet if she was going to need another surgery which would mean even more sling time, and then physio – yeah, it didn't seem to be worth asking yet, and they would ask.

And then there was Thor.

Emma remembered the first day she'd seen him, when Ainsley had bought him and the hauler had delivered him while Emma was in her weekly private lesson with Ainsley, riding Chico, the sweet chestnut Appendix Quarter Horse that had been her main ride before Thor. They'd been working in the outdoor arena, so she was able to stand by the fence, both Chico and herself very interested to see the big black warmblood backed down the ramp of the huge trailer, and led into the barn by Ainsley, who looked shorter than usual beside the tall horse. The trailer pulled out as soon as he was safely away, in a hurry to make their next delivery, and Emma had walked

Chico around the ring on a loose rein til Ainsley returned, enjoying the sunshine and daydreaming of the day when she might be able to ride such a big beautiful horse as that one.

It was sooner than she thought it would be, when Ainsley decided that she was going to focus on a different horse for her personal mount this season, and allowed Thor to be ridden by some of her upper level students. It took a while until she worked around to Emma, but she got her turn because some of the older girls were afraid of his headstrong ways, while others already had their own horses, or leased horses from Ainsley that they were committed to.

Thor didn't scare Emma, but no horse ever had. She was tall for her age, and having ridden anything Ainsley would let her since she was 7 years old meant that for half her life she'd been building the balance and strength to have confidence in the saddle. The first time she sat on Thor, Ainsley had exclaimed that her long legs suited him, and Emma had loved the power she felt in him. She laughed when he spooked at a corner, and was proud of her ability to hold him on course when he wanted to duck out at a jump.

Thor wasn't a horse that just anyone at the stable could ride, and Emma was proud that she was one who could. She was strong enough, and brave enough, and determined enough to keep him focused and going where she wanted.

Or she thought she was.

They'd had a lot of success together. In her bedroom at home a row of ribbons hung, all the ones since her very first schooling show on a pony named Coconut when she was just 7 years old, but there were twice as many won with Thor as any other horse.

Until the accident.

It wasn't really anything different than had happened dozens of other times – Thor tried to duck out on a jump, and she tried to make him go over it, but this time, it didn't work, and his balance failed him, and down he went.

Down they both went.

She would be able to get up again, eventually. Her shoulder would heal, with lots of help from the doctors and surgeons at the hospital. Already her concussion had improved – if they'd just give her the all-clear to have her phone back she'd nearly feel back to normal.

But Thor was still on stall rest. Thor was going to have to have more treatments. Thor might never be able to jump again.

A honking horn made her jump, she'd been so lost in thought. There was Ainsley stopped in the middle of the road in front of her house, in her big pickup and still pulling the horse trailer she'd used last night to pick up Thunder. Emma hurried down to climb in the passenger seat so Ainsley could move before too many neighbours became annoyed with their road being blocked.

"I could've called when I left Em, you didn't need to wait outside for me!" Ainsley looked worried, "I'm going to wear you out before I ever get you to the barn!"

"No that's okay, I was just daydreaming." Emma gave what she hoped was a reassuring smile.

"Sorry I'm late, didn't even get the trailer unhooked yet, Chico threw a shoe and he's got a clinic coming up this weekend with Taya so I had to squeeze him in when the farrier could do it, and of course it took longer than I hoped it would."

"No worries, I knew it would be something like that, there's always some horse crisis happening."

Ainsley laughed as Emma parroted back something she'd said so many times. "How is the little guy today? Did you get up to Ruby's to see him? Did you meet all the herd? Did you love Snickers? I just adore him, he's totally my first love. Oh, did you come up with a name yet?"

Emma answered the last question first. "I think so yeah, what do you think of Thunder?"

"I love it!" Ainsley said without hesitation. "It even goes with Thor, your other equine buddy!"

"Oh!" Emma looked at her in surprise. "I didn't even think of that! God of Thunder!"

"Thor and Thunder," Ainsley laughed delightedly, "It's perfect! And way better than Snookums."

Suddenly Emma remembered the photo of Ainsley with Snickers when she'd been even younger than Emma was now. "Hey, how come you never wear pink sparkly show shirts these days?"

"Oh no, she already showed you the album!?" Ainsley broke down in helpless giggles. "I knew it would happen sooner or later, but I was hoping for later!"

"That photo of Snickers jumping is amazing!" Emma said, "We need a copy for the tack room!"

"Maybe one day," Ainsley said, still giggling, "but I'm not sure I'm quite ready for new clients to know how little my very first jumping horse was."

"Why not? His form is perfect."

"That is true," said Ainsley, "Truly, the last 20 years has just been me trying to find a horse who was as talented and loved jumping as much as Snickers, only big enough to ride!" She paused, then added, "It's not Snickers I'm ashamed of, it's the pink and pigtails I'm not sure I'm ready to share with the world yet!"

Emma grinned. "I think you looked cute."

"Of course I did!" Ainsley pulled into the stable, and backed the trailer into its usual spot. "I'm always cute." She winked at Emma and slid out of the truck. "You go on in and see the big man, he's in his stall, and there's his favourite peppermints in the tack room, I'm going to unhook this trailer, which will probably mean I'll need it again later today, but you know, hope springs eternal." She made a goofy face and Emma laughed and left her to it, heading into the main door of the big stable.

Stone Ridge Stable was a beautiful place. It had two main barns, down either side of a huge, bright indoor riding arena. Emma glanced over at the even bigger outdoor sand ring, but it was empty today, most people preferring to ride inside this time of year, and of course it wasn't as busy at the barn midday like this. Ainsley leased the barn to the left of the arena for her clients and stable of lesson horses, while the other side was boarders, or sometimes a trainer rented a few stalls at a time.

Emma was almost on autopilot as she walked in and headed to the tack room to grab a handful of Thor's favourite peppermint candies. It was funny, some horses wouldn't even try them, but they were his very favourite treat, and she always gave him at least two – one when she first arrived and one while she was grooming him after she'd untacked him at the end of a ride. Today she took a whole handful and intended to give him every single one. He deserved some spoiling; it was the least she could do.

Coming out of the tack room she glanced at the blackboard, out of habit. The blackboard had the schedule on it – when lessons were booked, when the arena was free for open ride time, any notes from one boarder to another or updates and requests from the Ainsley or the barn owner, Brenda. But today, across the top in big letters it said, GET WELL SOON EMMA & THOR! and underneath were little notes written by it seemed like everyone in the barn.

Emma stopped midstride and stared, reading notes from Taya, Sarah and Maria, her closest barn friends, from the adult boarders she didn't know well, from Victoria, the snootiest girl in the barn, even from Brenda the barn owner, who usually didn't bother with even knowing the names of the riders, leaving all the interpersonal stuff to Ainsley. Some of the notes were getting a little scuffed, as it had been two weeks since the accident, but they must've left it all here for her to see, and Emma's eyes filled with tears as she thought of how she'd been worried about coming here and seeing these people, when they'd been so kind as to write such lovely well wishes to her. The notes said things like, "Heal fast!" "We miss you!" and "Get back in the saddle!" Emma wished her mom could see it, and reached for her phone to take a photo, until she remembered she didn't have it.

Four more days til she was out of the screentime ban.

She was still standing there, reading and rereading the messages when Ainsley came in from unhooking the trailer.

"Nice, eh?" Ainsley said when she walked up to her. "I was going to take a photo and send it to your mom to read it to you when you were in the hospital, but Maria suggested it would be nicer as a surprise when you got to come back."

"It's a great surprise!" Emma said with feeling. "Can you take a photo and send it to my mom though? She'd like to see too; I know she would."

"Of course!" Ainsley took her phone out of the back pocket of her breeches, snapped a photo, and Emma heard it make the whooshing sound of a sent message. "Done! Got the mints? Let's go see his highness!"

"Just a sec." Emma picked up the piece of chalk and wrote in in the middle of the board, in the biggest space she could find: THANK YOU ALL ♥ LOVE EMMA

Chapter 8

They walked together along the barn aisle to the familiar stall that had been Emma's destination when arriving at the barn for over a year now. Instead of a hand painted name sign like the stalls at the miniature horse farm, a magnetic whiteboard had THOR written in big block letters at the top, and then his AM and PM feed underneath, and at the bottom, a new addition of the words NO TURNOUT underlined three times, and underneath that Hand Walk Only, Cold Hose x2, and Banamine 12mL x1

Thor's big dark head wasn't hanging into the aisle over his stall gate like usual and Emma suddenly felt like there was a bowling ball dropped in the pit of her stomach. They drew closer and she could see his big shiny hip first. He was standing with his head low at the back corner of his stall, not eating hay, or watching the goings on in the barn aisle.

"Thor?" she said tentatively, and Ainsley echoed her, though her usual cheery tone sounded a bit forced to Emma.

"Thor, your Emma is here to see you!" Ainsley opened the latch and slid the big metal gate sideways to open it, and Thor turned his head to look, but he didn't lift it or spin around with the bolshy enthusiasm that Emma expected from him.

Emma looked down at the supportive bandages on both his front legs, in a bright cheerful yellow. "I thought he only hurt one leg? Why does he seem so quiet? Does he have a concussion or something like me?"

The questions came so fast that Ainsley held her hand up to slow the onslaught, and spoke very slowly for her, clearly trying sooth Emma's worries as she answered the questions in order. "He has an injury to his suspensory ligament on his left front. Both legs are bandaged to give the supporting limb some support as well, but there's nothing wrong with the right front whatsoever. He's fine otherwise, I think he's just a little dull with the stall rest, you know how he enjoys his turnout time to race around and be a loon, he's missing it, and is a bit sulky about it, but," Ainsley moved to make sure she was looking right into Emma's eyes, "He's going to be fine, and there was nothing you could've done better to keep it from happening. You both just need a bit of time and you'll be good as new, I promise." She reached over and squeezed Emma's hand, but it felt like she was squeezing her heart.

Emma knew she was trying to be reassuring, but standing there looking at Thor, looking dully at them and then turning his head back to the wall, she had trouble believing it. She nodded anyway, trying to look like she believed everything Ainsley was telling her.

"Get out those peppermints," Ainsley smiled her same old smile, but it did seem a little forced, "I bet just the sound of the plastic of the first one opening will perk him up!"

Emma did as she was told, and at the crinkle of the wrapper as she tore it open with her teeth there was a soft whicker from the big black horse and Ainsley stepped protectively in front of Emma, in case she got jostled by his hip as he spun around and began nosing around for his treat. Emma held it out to him on the palm of her hand and he lipped it up and twisted his head sideways, mouthing it around in that unique way he had, making you think he was really sucking on it for a while, until he got it between his teeth and you could hear the crunch. He savoured every bit, but in no time at all he asked for another and Emma was happy to oblige.

"See, he's the same old Thor now, isn't he?" Ainsley said, still providing a bit of a barrier between Thor's notorious lack of personal space and understanding of how large he was, and Emma's partially rebuilt shoulder. "And it's nearly time for his hand walk, he'll get to carefully stretch his legs. Jamie's been taking care of that because she's so tall and strong, he's a bit over excited when he gets out of that stall and we can't have him getting too crazy and risk hurting the leg, so she's been walking him in the indoor." Ainsley grinned, "Fresh air outside was a bit much for him, I took him the first day the vet said he was allowed a walk and I was pretty much flying him like a kite, couldn't get back inside fast enough!"

Emma had to giggle at the picture of flying a giant horse like a kite, but she was sad for Thor. He clearly wasn't enjoying his convalescence any more than she had been, before Thunder had come along to keep her interested and get her back up and at 'em.

She wondered how she could get Thor back up and at 'em.

Jamie came around the corner just then, carrying a heavy leather lead with a length of chain attached. They always used a chain on Thor, as he was so strong and seemed to have no concept of how strong he was. Many was the time that Emma was sure she never would've stopped him without that chain over his nose to remind him that she was there and trying to get his attention.

Jamie was the barn manager, and she was tall and broad and strong from decades of cleaning stalls and stacking hay and handling horses. She grinned when she saw Emma, her weathered face creasing underneath her battered ball cap.

"It's good to see you back, Emma, we've missed you around here! You're looking great, you must be healing like a champ!"

You couldn't help but smile back at Jamie, and Emma's was big and genuine, "The last couple days I am, I think, felt pretty slow before that though."

Jamie gestured to Thor who was reaching around Ainsley to nose at Emma's pocket. "I think it's the same with this one, he's been much brighter in his stall the last couple days, I know the vet's still worried, but I think he's feeling much better than he was."

Emma didn't know whether to feel reassured he was feeling better, or worried that he'd been worse than the dull staring at a wall she'd seen when she arrived. She watched as Jamie slipped his leather halter over his ears, and then threaded the chain through the rings to loop over his nose. Before she went out the stall she adjusted it once more, dropping the chain loop from over the bridge of his nose to slip through his mouth like a bit.

Emma was surprised, but as she followed Ainsley's direction to step out of the way and Thor charged out of the stall, she could see that only that chain and Jamie's strength and knowledge of how to use it kept him from getting loose and doing further damage to his injured tendon.

He snorted, much like Thunder when he was scared of something, and Emma wondered if Thor was scared. He made that noise a lot before he ducked out of a jump too. He'd made it before the accident, she remembered it clearly.

Was Thor scared?

Jamie used her weight on her right hand on the chain to keep Thor's head down, and used her left to hold up and block him from going straight to steer him through the open door to the indoor riding arena, and Emma followed at a safe distance, Ainsley holding firmly onto her good arm making sure she did, to see what happened when he got into the larger space.

When she came around the corner, Thor was rearing, standing tall on his hind legs, towering over Jamie and flailing his front legs, not at her exactly, but not really safely away from her either. Unconcerned, Jamie gave a few strong yanks on the lead, and the chain through his mouth seemed to get through to him and he alighted back on the ground and stood still. After a moment Jamie patted his neck, slipped the chain out of his mouth and back over his nose, and they began walking together around the perimeter, Thor now moving sedately and completely under control.

"See," Ainsley tucked her arm through Emma's as they watched him stride around the ring at Jamie's side, "he was just a bit sulky about his stall rest, he wouldn't be that rambunctious if he was feeling too badly!" Ainsley watched Thor seriously as he strode past them down the long side of the arena. "I think he looks better than yesterday, can barely see any lameness at the walk now."

Emma watched, and she couldn't see anything off about his gait, but she didn't have Ainsley's experience. He looked like himself, striding out at a big flowing walk, and Emma remembered what it felt like to just let him walk out like that, on the days that he would instead of spooking or charging off on her into a faster gait.

Ainsley looked at her watch. "Do you mind if I run you home Emma? I've got a lesson to teach in half an hour, wow, time flies doesn't it!"

"Sure," Emma said, "I'm a bit tired, actually, that sounds good." She was tired, exhausted really, but she wasn't sure if it was from activity and her injuries or worry over Thor.

"Wait!" Ainsley said as Emma turned to leave the arena. She flagged down Jamie and Thor as they went past, and had Emma stand with them for a photo. "For your mom!" Ainsley said as she snapped the pic, "Emma and Thor, reunited!"

Emma took the chance to slip Thor another peppermint, but he didn't seem to enjoy it as much as the earlier ones, and returned to walking his laps without any real enthusiasm, not even looking around him. It was like when Jake had finally caught Thunder, and suddenly all the life went out of him.

Emma walked out to Ainsley's truck for the short ride home. She couldn't put her finger on exactly what was bothering her, but something was. It wasn't just worry for Thor, but this feeling that something was wrong with the way they'd handled him, like something was wrong with little Thunder being manhandled and dragged around. She didn't know what the answer was, or really even the question but ... something was wrong.

"I did wear you out," Ainsley said, looking over worriedly, "you're so quiet, are you okay?"

Emma smiled at her to reassure her. "I'm fine, it's just been a busy couple days after two weeks of laying around doing nothing but healing, it's worn me out is all! But it was worth it, thank you for coming to get me so I could see Thor, I really appreciate it."

"I'll let you know the next time I have a window of opportunity and I'll come fetch you again if you'd like!"

"That'd be great, thanks – only four more days and I get my phone back, and you can text me!" Emma said.

"I'll send you a Thor photo every day as soon as you do!"

Emma climbed up the front steps, punched the door code, and turned to wave at Ainsley who'd waited to be sure she got in before pulling away. She looked at the clock as she closed the door behind her. Still a couple hours before her mom would be home.

The recliner was calling. She really was exhausted, and she grabbed a blanket and fell asleep in no time flat.

A dreamless sleep.

Thank goodness.

Chapter 9

"Em?" Her mom spoke softly, and her touch on Emma's forehead was gentle, but Emma awoke with a jerk and then winced and grabbed her shoulder. "I'm sorry, I'm sorry!" said Mom, "I was trying not to startle you and I did it anyway."

"It's okay," Emma took a deep breath, wincing as she waited for the pain to fade. Her mom held out a hand containing her pain pills and picked up a glass of water she'd set on the side board. Emma took the pills, popped them in her mouth, drank the entire glass of water and said, "Thank you!"

"Wow." Mom looked at the empty water glass. "I take it you didn't hydrate that well today?"

Emma thought. "I had a root beer at Ruby's, and a coke with lunch."

"Of course you did." Mom went back to the kitchen, filled the glass again, and handed it to her. "Drink. Your healing brain needs to be hydrated."

Emma did as she was told, then flopped back in the recliner. She was still tired, even though she must've slept for at least two hours.

"You've been overdoing it the last couple days." Mom's eyebrows were drawn together in concern as she looked down at her, then sank onto the nearby couch. "You don't move for the rest of today, and I think you better stay home tomorrow and rest."

Emma wanted to argue, but she really was tired. And sore. "Maybe you're right. Could we just run over to see Thunder when you get home from work tomorrow night maybe? For a minute?"

"If you're feeling up to it," Mom agreed, "I'd kinda like to see the little guy again myself! Did you have a good visit today? Did everyone think Thunder was the right name?"

"Yes!" Emma felt a little more energetic talking about Thunder. "Everyone agreed that it's a great name for him, and he almost took a treat from my hand!"

"Were you careful?" Mom frowned at her.

Emma rolled her eyes, "YES, I was on the other side of the fence sitting in a chair." And then she shared the whole story, about tossing him treats and how his whiskers touched her hand, and about the other Miniature Horses, and the photos of Ainsley when she was a little girl.

"I hope you're up to it tomorrow afternoon," Mom said, "Because I can't wait to meet the rest of the herd!" She pointed at Emma. "You do some good resting tomorrow, okay?" She winked and Emma agreed solemnly.

"I got the photos from Ainsley!" Mom got up to go get her phone from the table by the front door, and opened it to the photo of Emma with Thor and Jamie. "Thor looks great! Was he happy to see you?"

Emma made a face. "Not at first. He just stood at the back of his stall, but he came over when he realized I had peppermints."

Mom laughed. "He does love his peppermints!"

Emma was serious. "Ainsley says he's fine, just sulky about having to stay in the stall, but I'm worried about him. He doesn't seem like himself, and then he was so crazy when Jamie took him out, she had to put the chain through his mouth so he wouldn't get away and hurt his leg again."

"Oh, I'm sure he'll be okay Em." Mom reached over and pushed her hair back from her face. "You were getting a little grumpy on your 'stall rest' too until you went for a walk and met a wild pony!"

Emma managed a half smile. "I guess I'm still kinda tired and cranky." Then a thought came to her, and her smile turned genuine. "Maybe Thor needs a Miniature Horse too!"

Mom laughed. "I'm afraid he'd accidentally stomp one! Like an ant – his big feet might not even notice it was there!"

Emma giggled. "Maybe not then." She sobered. "But I do wish I knew a way to make him feel better about his stall rest. Because I think it's going to be longer than mine, because they can't put his leg in a sling and tell him not to use it."

"Let's stop at the tack store tomorrow evening," Mom suggested, "maybe we can find a toy or treat or something that would help keep him busy?"

"Oh!" Emma brightened up. "That's a great idea, thanks Mom! I'll nap all day so I'm sure to feel well enough!"

***

Emma was true to her word, and after sleeping all night long, she slept off and on most of the day too. Apparently when you are recovering from surgery and a concussion then two busy days in a row, it takes a LOT of sleep to recover, she thought.

When she was awake, she was thinking.

Thinking about how to make friends with Thunder, and what it really meant to be friends with a horse.

Then thinking about Thor. If someone had asked her she'd have said they were friends, but he didn't even look when she'd come to the gate at first.

And about that snorting noise they both made, like a fire breathing dragon.

When Thunder made it he was scared, no doubt about it, but Thor did it all the time. Did that mean Thor was scared too?

It was at the same time as he spooked in the corner or ducked and refused a jump, and her instructors had always told her he was being bad, "evading" was the word they used. Did "evading" mean the same as "scared"? And if he was scared, was making him do it the right way to make him less scared? Or the right way to be his friend?

Emma shook her head. Maybe she had too much time for thinking right now, and was making it more complicated than she needed to.

She went to the kitchen for a glass of water, determined to do everything she could to feel up to visiting Thunder and the tack store tonight, and then tucked herself back in the big recliner under a fuzzy blanket and went back to sleep.

There were no complicated questions to worry about while she was asleep.

***

When Emma's mom walked through the door after work Emma was up and dressed and hydrated, waiting for her.

"Well!" Mom set her bag down on the hall table. "You have done a good job resting today, you look perkier than I feel!"

"I napped all day," Emma said proudly, "and I drank six glasses of water."

"Good girl," Mom hung up her work coat and put her shoes in the closet. "Just give me fifteen minutes to change and take a breath and then we'll go."

Emma gave her a hug. "Thank you, Mom!"

In no time they were in the car headed down the road to Cool Waters Miniature Horse Farm. Mom did the same as Granny and pulled right up to Thunders paddock. They paused before they got out of the car, as Thunder was trotting back and forth, watching because the horses across the yard were bucking and playing together. He whinnied at them, then took off across his pen, bucking and leaping around, and then he put his long white tail straight in the air, like that fancy Arabian on the other side of the Stable at Stone Ridge, and trotted across in front of him, tossing his long mane, his thick tail like a proud flag flying behind him while his knees snapped up in front of him and he floated across the ground.

"Wow." Mom said exactly what Emma was thinking. "I don't think even Thor can float like that!"

A knock at Emma's window made them both jump, so captivated they'd been by the show that Thunder was putting on. Emma scrambled to open the window when she looked up to Ruby's smiling face.

"He's giving you quite the show, isn't he?" Ruby said, her own eyes on the horse instead of Emma.

"He's beautiful," Emma watched him, looking like he was in slow motion in real life as he hung in the air in a moment of suspension between every step of first the trot, and then the canter.

"He looks like a deer bouncing like that!" Emma's mom sounded amazed.

"The wind come up a few minutes ago," Ruby said, "and started them all going. I was just coming out to try to get a video for you," Ruby showed the phone in her hand, "Good thing you came when you did, I'm not that good at videoing, might've got my own face instead!" She leaned close conspiratorially, her eyes still on Thunder. "It's happened before, my boys laughed so hard."

"Mom! Take a video!" Emma said, but her mom was already digging through her purse for her phone with one hand and opening the car door with the other.

She just got the phone up and pointed in Thunder's direction when he gave one last big buck, went past in the big tail flagging floating trot, made one of his dragon snorts, and stopped near his hay. He stood with his head high, eyes and nostrils wide, silvery mane blowing in the wind as he looked over towards the other Miniature Horses.

"A picture of that, I need a picture," Emma's mom mumbled to herself as she fumbled with the phone.

Thunder blew one more time, then seemed to decide the excitement was over and dropped his head back to his hay.

"Did you get it Mom?" Emma asked excitedly.

"I'm not sure," she handed Emma the phone, then pulled it back just as she reached for it, "wait no, you're not supposed to be looking at screens that close."

Emma rolled her eyes. She really didn't think a quick look at the video and photos would make the difference in her recovery, but she was too happy having seen the show Thunder put on in real life to be too annoyed. He was so beautiful, and he was hers!

"I got the big buck and a few strides of the trot!" Emma's mom said triumphantly, sounding a little surprised, "and this photo!" She held the phone for Emma to see, holding it out of reach like Emma might grab it and hold it to her eyeball for an hour, exacerbating her concussion.

But when Emma saw it, she thought it might've been a possibility – it was so beautiful, the wire of the fence was in the way, but you could see his beautiful blue eyes, his dished face, and that amazing mane. "He looks like a model in a wind machine!" Emma said, and Ruby laughed and agreed.

"Mother Nature's wind machine!"

Emma got out of the car, and Mother Nature's wind machine grabbed her hair, flinging it across her face so she couldn't really see for a moment. "I wonder how Thunder sees through all that mane!"

"I wonder that about my guys sometimes," Ruby said, "but they never seem to mind."

Emma went over to her chair, still waiting by the gate and sat down, and Thunder lifted his head and looked at her curiously.

"He's more interested in you right away than he was yester-day!" Ruby said encouragingly, "He remembers you were the source of those yummy cookies." She gestured under the chair. "I put that little tub of cookies there, that way it has a lid so the birds can't steal them and the weather can't get them, but they'll be there in case you come to visit when I'm not home."

Emma reached under to slide the square plastic tub out and popped the lid off. "Thank you, Ruby!"

"Yes," Emma's mom echoed, "Thank you so much, that's very thoughtful."

Emma took out a treat and tossed it towards Thunder, who had backed off a few steps at the sound of the tub scraping the ground, but the wind caught the treat and instead of it falling at his feet it landed some distance from him.

He never hesitated though, walking right over to where it had fallen and eating it up, chewing cheerfully while he threw his head up and watched Emma, clearly wondering if she would throw another.

And, of course, she did.

This one also went off course and away he went after it, lengthening his walk to hurry along.

"He likes this game!" Emma's mom said, "I mean, so would I though, I'd chase a cookie too!"

"Some horses struggle with following a treat though," Ruby said, "of course they want the cookie, everyone likes cookies, but they aren't like dogs who are comfortable with tracking a moving object like that. After all, their food is usually sitting still! Thunder is a smartie pants, he's caught onto this so fast."

This time Emma didn't throw the cookie as far, thinking it both might not get caught by the wind and might bring him closer to her, and was right on both counts. Thunder didn't even hesitate, closing the distance between them until he was just two arms lengths away.

This time Emma barely dropped the treat past the end of her fingers, then froze and did her best not to move as he approached to take it, a bit more cautious now, his blue eyes watching her for any sign that he might need to run. He moved slowly, breathing big huffing breaths – but no dragon noises, Emma thought happily – until he got his nose to the treat, lipped it up, and backed away to chew it, but only a step or two. Emma thought that was a good step and reached for another treat, trying to keep her movements quiet and steady.

This time she left the treat on the flat of her hand, extended towards him as far as she could reach, with the treat on her fingers so it was as close to him as she could get it.

Thunder looked at her, still chewing the last treat, and she would swear he was considering. But he didn't move, didn't step towards her or stretch his neck out or even make a dragon snort.

Emma waited. She had the feeling he was waiting to see what she would do, like he thought she was setting a trap for him.

Still he stood and watched her from underneath his thick forelock.

Emma's arm began to ache, but he hadn't lost interest, so she didn't quite feel like it was time to give up and toss him the treat. As long as he was still standing there giving her his attention she thought it was worth waiting. She would've liked to ask Ruby what she thought but she knew Ruby wasn't saying anything to avoid startling him, so she thought she better not either, and just sat there, barely daring to breathe.

But then she remembered.

Yesterday, she'd talked to him. She'd thought it was silly, and was glad no one had seen her, but maybe he liked it. Maybe it had helped.

"It's okay, Thunder," she kept her voice low, but his ears pricked even more forward and she knew he was listening. "I won't grab you, I couldn't if I wanted to from this side of the fence. My arm can't reach any further and actually it's getting super tired trying to hold this treat for you. All you have to do is walk over and pick it up and I promise not to do anything scary at all. I'd just be very excited if you took a treat from my hand because it would feel like we were getting to be friends. What do you think, Thunder, do you think we can be friends?" Emma paused for breath, and Thunder worked his lips like he was thinking about the taste of that cookie. Emma couldn't hold her breath now, she'd talked away all her oxygen and holding her arm out that long wasn't easy, so she instead tried to take deep slow breaths that she hoped wouldn't upset him, and while she was thinking all this, Thunder blinked, dropped his head, walked forward, and took the treat off her hand. "Good boy!" Emma breathed without thinking, and hoped it hadn't scared him, but it didn't seem to. She dropped her hand (gratefully) and he still didn't move, chewing his cookie thoughtfully, and then meandering a short distance away without hurrying.

Emma took three treats and tossed them his way, telling him in a more normal voice, "Good Boy!" and then she stood up to turn around and celebrate with her mom and Ruby.

"Did you see!? He took it from my hand!"

"See it?" Ruby said, "your mom got it on video!"

"Did you really? Can I see?" Emma grabbed the phone and this time her mom let her take it and bring up the video. It was almost more exciting to watch it over again. Emma gave a little squeal and jumped up and down, then worried she might've scared Thunder and whirled around to see, but he was back at his hay, watching her a bit curiously, but not with any fear in his eyes.

Her mom went and looked in the tub of treats. "What kind are these that he likes so much? We can get him some more at the tack store." She snapped the lid on and slid it back under the folding chair.

Ruby told her the brand name. "Will you be out tomorrow?"

Emma looked at her mom hopefully. "'Fraid not, Em," her mom shook her head sadly, "tomorrow we're back at the hospital to get an x-ray and ultrasound of that shoulder to see how you're healing, and I suspect that'll be enough excitement for one day."

Emma sighed and went back to the fence to talk to Thunder for a minute. "I can't come see you tomorrow Thunder, but I'll be back the next day. Don't worry, I haven't left you, I'm still your friend." She looked around at Ruby. "Do you think he understands me?"

"Not your words," Ruby said, "But he's an expert at understanding your tone and your intentions. You keep right on talking to him, he understands enough to make it well worth it."

"I feel kinda silly," she said, "no one talks to their horses at the barn like that, or at least, not while anyone is around."

"Do you think it helped?" Ruby asked.

"Yes! My arm was getting tired, and I remembered last time he'd come up and tried to take the treat I was talking to him, so I thought I'd try it again and it worked!"

"Then I think that his is the only opinion that really matters, isn't it?" Ruby's eyes crinkled as she smiled, looking between Emma and Thunder. "I think you made a big step in your friendship today, and he'll be pleased to see you when you come back in a couple days."

Ruby waved them off, telling them to have fun shopping.

At the tack store, Emma went straight to the horse treats, searching until she found the brand that they knew Thunder liked, and then she talked her mom into two more kinds to try too, in case he liked those better, and so they'd have enough to share with Thor.

Next, they asked the nice girl who worked there about things that might help a horse who was on stall rest, and she brought them to a shelf with a whole selection of hanging toys and treats for him to lick and nibble on to keep him busy.

"Look Mom! It's peppermint flavour!" Emma held up a big circular hanging thing that looked vaguely like a lifesaver.

"Well, that must be the one to try then, it's meant to be."

By the time they'd gathered their shopping, Emma was getting tired again and she stared at the bulletin board near the till while they were ringing up their items.

"Food rewards" Emma read, and then started paying attention and read the whole flyer.

Positive Reinforcement Training for Horses

Clinic Sold Out but Auditing available - $30/person

Learn the benefits of using food rewards in your horse training.

And there was a date this coming weekend and the name of a stable nearby where Emma had attended clinics before.

"Mom!" She pulled on her mom's sleeve, earning a startled look as she'd interrupted her chatting with the staff member quite rudely, "Mom look! This might help Thunder! It's only $30 to audit, can we go, please can we go?"

"It looks great, Em, but I can't, I traded days to get tomorrow off for your appointment, so I'm working on Saturday." Emma sagged with disappointment, but her mom took a photo of the flier. "Maybe Granny will go with you? We'll see what we can come up with, but I'm not sure you are quite up to sitting in a barn all day – we'll check with the doctor tomorrow and see what he says."

Emma crossed her fingers. It seemed like it was meant to be, just what she needed to learn more about how to be friends with Thunder, and teach him things without him being so scared all the time or trying to drag her and get away from her.

"Come on," said her mom, "we'll drop a little care package for Thor at Stone Ridge on the way home."

Chapter 10

Emma struggled to keep her eyes open in the uncomfortable waiting room chair, thinking that she probably would be asleep if it wasn't that her shoulder was aching from being moved around for x-rays and ultrasounds. Seriously, they tell her to keep the sling on pretty much 100% of the time for two weeks and then they get it out and wrench it around. Ouch.

"Emma?" A lady in bright pink scrubs stood in the door holding a clipboard and Emma and her mom stood up and followed her out of the waiting room and up the hallway to the exam rooms. They had to rush; the lady with the clipboard was in a hurry and they sped up as she turned a corner ahead of them.

She stopped in front of an open door with a big smile in their direction. "Have a seat and the doctor will be with you soon!" She slid the clipboard into the slot on the door and was disappearing off down the hall again before they'd made a move into the room.

"Wow," Emma's mom said, "I'm guessing she's not the reason we're already an hour late."

Emma gave a half hearted giggle. She plunked herself in yet another hospital chair, though this one was a bit more padded than the one in the waiting room had been. She yawned. "A day of hospital diagnostics and appointments is way more exhausting than a day of 'pony shenanigans'."

Her mom yawned too. "Stop that, yawning is contagious, now we'll just sit here and yawn at each other and the doctor will be greeted by our tonsils when she comes in."

They yawned in unison, and giggled.

"You're right though," Mom said, "I don't think there's much more exhausting than a day of medical appointments, but the painful ones are done at least, just talk to this doctor about your shoulder and one more about your noggin and then we go home." She yawned again. "To bed," she said, and stuck her tongue out at Emma, who was, of course, yawning again.

"But," Emma said through the last of her yawn, "This could be painful too, if this doctor says, 'nope your shoulder is still broken, gotta try again,' and then that doctor says, 'nope your brain is still broken, gotta lay in the dark for a week, no more fresh air and ponies for you!'"

"I have a good feeling about your concussion, don't you?" Her mom asked her, looking a bit anxious.

"Oh yeah," Emma said, nodding more vigorously than necessary to demonstrate her ability to do so without inducing a headache. "My head hasn't ached the last couple days, and I think the last time it did it was because I was dehydrated."

Mom looked at her intently. "And did we learn anything from that?"

Emma rolled her eyes, which, for the record, also didn't give her a headache. "Yes, Mom."

"Just maybe try not to let this doctor see the rope burn," Mom said, wrinkling her nose and Emma peered at the shiny area on her right hand.

"It's healing good," she said, "doesn't hurt any-" she trailed off abruptly as the doorknob turned, and quickly closed her hand into a fist and tucked it into the pocket of her sweater, trying not to look too guilty as she smiled a greeting at the kind surgeon who had put her shoulder back together for her.

"How are you feeling, Emma!" Dr. Wall spoke enthusiastically and looked at Emma with a measuring gaze. "You look quite well."

"Yes, pretty good," Emma said, "The shoulder is still pretty sore, it didn't like moving around for x-rays very much."

Dr. Wall made a sympathetic face. "I know, that's the worst. How's your pain management? Is the protocol we sent you home on keeping you comfortable?"

Mom answered for her. "Yes, but we sure do notice when she's due for more, don't we Em?"

Emma nodded.

"Yeah, we won't be reducing those pain meds anytime soon, there's still a lot of healing to do, but-" Dr. Wall paused and turned the tablet in her hands towards them to show the x-rays, "it is healing well! I think we're going to be able to avoid another surgery at this rate!"

"Yay!" Emma said, and then tried to pay attention while the doctor explained why that was and pointed at the xray and ultrasound images that looked like nothing but blurry grey and black bits to her. She remembered that Ainsley said Thor had an ultrasound on his injured leg, and suspected that if she saw Thor's ultrasound, and hers, side by side she would have no idea which was which.

"It's good news Emma," said Dr. Wall, drawing Emma's attention back to what she was saying, "But we're not out of the woods. You still need to be very careful – any sort of a fall or pull on that shoulder at this point could put us right back to square one and guarantee another surgery, and another injury at this point could even impact your long term range of motion, and you want to keep using that shoulder for a long time to come."

Emma nodded and tried to look solemn, like she would never ever grab the lead of a runaway pony while healing from a serious shoulder injury.

"I know you're a horse girl," Dr. Wall continues, "and I've repaired enough joints belonging to horse girls to know that you're itching to get back in the saddle, so I'm going to say this expressly – no riding for the foreseeable future." She held up a hand as though to fend off an argument she thought was coming, but Emma found she didn't want to argue. "We aren't even going to put a timeline on it at this point, because we want it to be Capital H Healed before we even start talking about it, okay?" She looked at Emma closely. "I know that's probably disappointing for you, I'm sorry."

"No, it's okay," Emma said. "I want my shoulder to get better. I can wait." She hesitated, and then asked, "Can I do other things with horses? Grooming and leading and stuff?"

"Grooming, yes, as long as it's a quiet horse that isn't going to crash into you. A quiet horse AND with an adult present." Dr. Wall ticked the options off on her fingers as she answered them. "Leading, I don't think so, not yet, not even a quiet horse, as I've repaired quite a few shoulders that were injured just by a normally docile horse getting scared of something."

"What about just interacting with them from the other side of a fence?" Emma's mom asked, and Emma looked anxiously for the answer.

"That's perfect," said the doctor, "having that fence between you and nothing attached between you and the horse is ideal to keep you safe and still be able to interact with them. That's my official horse time recommendation! Any other questions?"

Emma shook her head, and started wondering about what other ways she could play with Thunder without going in the pen with him.

Back in the car in the hospital parkade, Emma's mom made a little drumroll on the steering wheel, pulled Emma's phone out of her purse and handed it to her. "Early parole!"

Emma grinned and took the phone, hitting the power button to turn it on. "That was the best news we got all day!" she said, "Can I have your phone too? I want to send myself those photos and videos of Thunder."

Emma's mom cheerfully handed over her phone as well, then started the car. "Seatbelt on," she said, and Emma set the phones on the dash while she wrangled the seatbelt one handed. She was getting better at that – it still wasn't easy but she could do it without help now.

"I think this calls for a celebration," Emma's mom said as she went down the ramp out of the parking complex. "Also, I'm starving. We have totally missed lunch after waiting for all those appointments. What would you like for a celebratory early supper?"

Emma thought for only a few seconds. "Pizza!" she said, then added, "and cake!"

"Cake?" Her mom looked over surprised.

"Well, you said it was a celebration!" Emma shrugged her good shoulder.

Mom laughed. "You got it." She turned on the signal light to pull onto the main road away from the hospital. "You use your newly restored screentime privileges to order pizza for pickup and I'll run into the grocery store for a cake. And then call Granny, and give her all the updates and invite her over for pizza and cake!"

***

"I knew the minute that Emma's number came up on my phone that you'd gotten good news!" Granny said, giving Emma a hug and then reaching for a plate and helping herself to pizza.

Emma and her mom hadn't waited for her, they were too hungry. Emma wondered if she had room for one more piece of pizza, and then decided to wait for cake.

"We did." Emma's mom said, "but the surgeon who fixed her shoulder was very clear that there's to be no horsing around for a while, or the consequences could be dire." She pointed at Emma.

"No!" Emma said, "She said I could interact with them however I wanted from the other side of a fence."

"That's good," Granny said, going to the fridge to help herself to a can of her favourite sparkling water that they always kept for her. "You can keep playing the cookie game with Thunder then!"

"And there must be lots of other things I can do through a fence," Emma got her phone out and googled 'how to work with a horse through a fence' but then frowned as she scrolled through articles about teaching them to jump, or building safe fences for horse pastures, and lots about a sport called 'reined cow horse.' "I don't think I'm asking the right question."

"Speaking of the right question," Mom pointed a piece of pizza at Emma as she put it on her plate. "don't you have something to ask your Granny about tomorrow?"

"Oh!" Emma set her phone down on the table. "Do you have a busy day tomorrow, Granny? Mom has to work, but I saw a flier at the tack store for a clinic all about using treats to train horses, and I think it's just what I need to learn more about how to teach Thunder stuff, because he already loves treats but Mom can't go, so do you think you could take me? Just for a while even? You don't have to stay, it's at the Green's barn, I've been to lots of clinics there before, I'd be fine on my own if you just wanted to drop me and pick me up later, especially now I have my phone again."

Granny held up her hand at the onslaught of words and set her pizza back on her plate. "Just a minute," she said, laughing as she pushed her chair back, "you know I have no idea what I'm doing without my calendar in front of me." She got up and went to the hall table to get her phone out of her purse, and came back to sit down, frowning at it. "What time did you say you wanted to be there?"

Emma looked at her mom, who got her own phone out to check the flyer they'd taken a photo of. "It's from 9-4," she said, "but Em, I don't think you better plan to be there that long anyway, that's too big a day for someone who's still supposed to be resting and healing. Maybe you could choose either morning or afternoon? Depending on Granny's schedule."

"Granny's schedule," said Granny, apologetically, "is pretty busy tomorrow. You know how Saturdays can be for me, I have an open house all morning and 3 showings in the afternoon, plus one in the evening." Emma's face fell with disappointment. "But," Granny said, and Emma brightened up hopefully, "If you didn't mind coming to my first afternoon showing with me, I could then drop you off at 2, and pick you up again at 4." She looked up from her phone at Emma. "I know that's not much of the clinic, but it's the best I can do tomorrow, sorry lovey."

Emma shoved her chair back to go give her a hug. "That's awesome Granny, thanks! I'm sure I can learn a ton in two hours." Emma reached for the pizza, forgetting she'd decided to save room for cake. But it didn't matter, she was going to learn something that would help Thunder and, besides, there was always room for cake.

Chapter 11

Emma spent the following morning carefully packing herself a bag for the clinic (water bottle, a new notebook and colourful pens, a granola bar for snacking, extra pain meds, a sweater), and catching up with messages on her phone. She sent the photos and video of Thunder to Ainsley (who responded with 'OH EM GEE' and a reciprocal photo of Thor, tongue out, about to take a peppermint off her hand), Maria from the barn ('aww'), Taya from the barn ('he almost looks like a real horse lol'), and Ashley from school ('it's a tiny horsey, so cute!' and then a long story about English class that Emma didn't really follow having missed more than two weeks of school and being completely out of the loop of all the recent high school drama).

And then she took a nap. She wanted to be fully refreshed and ready to learn, and while initially she thought she wouldn't sleep, she was so excited by the unknown possibilities for learning, it turns out that healing really did take a lot of energy and the next thing she knew Granny was gently shaking her awake.

"Are you all right, lovey?" Granny looked down at the recliner with concern. "If you're not up to it, you can stay home, there will be other clinics, I'm sure."

"No!" Emma sat up quickly, rubbing her eyes. "I'm fine, I was just trying to get some extra sleep so I'll be rested up and ready to learn this afternoon. Didn't expect to sleep so long though, sorry!"

"You sure?" Granny still looked skeptical.

"Yep!" Emma scurried out of the room to run a brush through her hair and grab her pre-packed bag. "I'll be ready in less than two minutes!" she called back to Granny.

"You hungry?" Granny asked, as they headed out the door. "Because I could go for some McNuggets."

Emma chose to sit in the car during Granny's first showing of the afternoon. She got out her note book and wrote POSITIVE REINFORCEMENT CLINIC at the top of the first page, then underneath: Questions about Thunder. 1. How do I use treats to make friends with him? 2. Can I use treats to teach him to lead without dragging me and running off? 3. What can I teach him from the other side of the fence?

Emma chewed thoughtfully on a cold french fry. She could come up with a zillion more questions, but she thought that was a good place to start. She knew she was probably going to miss the part in the morning where they really, properly explained all the basics, as that's usually how clinics worked, but hopefully she'd be able to figure out a good starting point towards answering her questions by watching the afternoon sessions.

Granny was back much sooner than Emma expected. "Are you done already?"

"Yeah," Granny started the car, "Just looky loos, not really right for them, and they have a bunch more houses to see." She glanced at her watch before she backed out of the driveway. "Looks like I'm going to get you there closer to 1:30 than 2."

"Yay!" Emma danced in her seat, "I've got my notebook all ready to fill with new things to learn!"

It took no time to drive to the stable where the clinic was, and Granny had to call, "Wait!" to stop Emma before she leapt out of the car. "You got your phone?" Emma pointed at her pocket. "Good. Be careful, call if you need anything, and I'll text you after my next showing to make sure you're doing okay." Emma nodded. "Okay, I'll see you at 4, unless I hear otherwise. Have fun, learn lots!"

"I will!" Emma waved and then put her bag over her shoulder and headed into the big building. She knew the way to the arena, from her previous visits here, but was stopped just inside the door by a smiling middle aged lady sitting at a table.

"Are you here to audit the clinic?"

"Yes!" Emma fumbled in her pocket for the cash her mom had sent with her, "$30, right?"

"Since you're only here for the afternoon, it's just $15, and I'll just get you to put your name on the list here."

"Great!" Emma pocketed the extra $15 and wrote her name as directed.

"Are you new to positive reinforcement training?" the lady asked conversationally as she tucked the money into a cashbox.

"Yes," said Emma, "I don't know anything about it, really, but I have a new Miniature Horse who I think it would work really well for. I'm so excited to learn all about it, but I couldn't get a ride this morning."

"I'm sure you'll get a lot out of this afternoon's sessions," the lady said with a smile. "And there's even a Miniature Horse in one of them too!"

"Really!" Emma adjusted her bag and inched towards the arena. She didn't want to miss anything important while she was chatting with the registration lady.

"Enjoy the clinic!" The lady said, and Emma made her escape, hurrying down the barn aisle and carefully going through to the bleachers at the end of the arena.

She tried to be as quiet as possible and not disturb those who were already sitting watching, but especially not the horses who were in the arena learning. She went all the way to the top row, found a spot far from any of the other spectators who were auditing the clinic, and then immediately rummaged into her bag, pulling out her notebook, pens and water bottle, and got herself all settled with her bag on the hard wooden bench on one side of her, the unicorn-themed water bottle and the extra pens on the other side, and notebook in her lap.

Clicking the pen and opening the notebook, poised to write, she looked up into the arena for the first time.

And her mouth dropped open in surprise at what she saw.

Emma had been to lots of clinics. They were all pretty much the same. A rider, or two or three riders, rode around the edge of the arena, or over poles or jumps, while the instructor walked around and gave instructions over a loud speaker, or sometimes didn't even walk, instead sitting in a chair and directing and making corrections from there.

What she saw in the arena now was entirely different.

There was a round pen set up in the middle of the arena, but it wasn't like the round pens that Emma had seen before, made out of solid panels to keep horses in. Instead it was just made of a single row of brightly striped plastic poles, somehow balanced on top of tall orange traffic cones.

And usually a round pen was made to contain a horse, so that you could direct them and move them more easily, but in this case, the horse was outside the poles, free in the arena, and didn't have a speck of tack on, while the two humans in the arena were inside the pen.

One human, clearly the instructor, wore a headset microphone, while the other held a ... feather duster?

Emma definitely wished she'd been there in the morning.

Or maybe not. Because this all looked crazy.

She listened to what the instructor was saying, but it didn't seem to help clarify anything right away. She was talking about balance, and bending in the direction of travel, which sounded very familiar to Emma. That part could've been straight from one of the dressage clinics she'd taken, but it didn't explain the feather duster, or the fact that the humans were in the pen chatting while the horse wandered around the arena, nosing through the dirt.

"All right!" The instructor said brightly, "Let's give it a try, show him the target, and get few good repetitions before you try movement."

The student walked to the edge of the pen near the horse, and held out the feather duster towards him. Emma watched in amazement as the horse promptly lifted his head, walked over with his ears up, and put his muzzle on the feather duster. There was a sharp clicking sound, and then the student reached into a pouch she wore around her waist, and gave the horse something that he ate eagerly. She held out the duster again, higher this time, and the horse reached his nose up to touch it, the click sounded – Emma looked closely and realized the clicker was attached to the handle of the duster – and the horse was fed.

"He's really caught on to that target since this morning, hasn't he?" The instructors voice interrupted Emma's hyper-focus on trying to see what the heck was going on.

Feather Duster = Target Emma scribbled in her notebook.

The third time, when the duster was placed close to the horse's chest, he took a step back in order to drop his head and touch it, and once again the student clicked the clicker when he did, and fed him what looked like a handful of small pellets, like the alfalfa pellets that Thor got as part of his grain ration.

"Okay!" The instructor's voice came over the loudspeaker, "walk along the round pen, and present the target, but remember, this time we're not clicking when he touches the target, but instead we're reinforcing movement."

Reinforcing movement? Emma had no idea what that meant, but watched intently to see what was going to happen.

The student walked along the barrier of the strange little round pen, and the horse, a leggy bay with a big lopsided star, watched her go, chewing thoughtfully on the last handful of pellets she'd given him. With some prompting from the instructor, she held out the target and the horse stepped out eagerly to come touch it. As soon as he was walking out along the edge of the pen, she clicked, and he continued on to where she stood to feed him.

The next time when she walked off, the horse almost immediately began to walk, so they were walking together around the pen, the horse on the outside, the human on the inside.

Next, the instructor had the student back into the middle of the circle, and then go forward and meet the horse further along the pen to reinforce him.

Reinforce = food. Emma wrote in her notebook.

When the student tried it, walking from edge to middle to edge again, like she was tracing one piece of pizza out of the whole, then feeding the horse when she got to the edge each time, the horse was walking very comfortably along the perimeter, and would start walking as soon as the handler began fading away from the edge, as he knew she would meet him with food further along the circle.

"Now," said the instructor, addressing herself to the audience as well as the active student, "You can see what I was talking about, how the reverse round pen sets them up for better balance in movement right from the beginning, unlike circling on a lunge line."

Emma looked and she *could* see; he was bent in the same direction as the circle, which is what good bend was, according to her dressage lessons. Then she pictured Thor on the lunge line, head up in the air and bent away from her as he pulled against the line, even with a chain on as well. Yeah, much better balance in this case!

"Also," the instructor was saying, "like we were talking about this morning, we now have a repeatable behaviour – walking – that we could start to put on a verbal cue. That would be the next step, but instead, let's just play a little more and see if we can get a trot from him." She directed the handler to make her pizza slices bigger, so the horse had further of the pen to get around to meet her with his food reward.

It only took three tries before he broke into a few steps of trot to get there sooner, and when the handler clicked the trot, the next time he trotted nearly right away and all the way until she got to him.

Soon the horse was trotting happily around the strange little round pen, and the instructor reminded them all to look at his balance again, and once again Emma contrasted it to Thor, because that was the horse she'd lunged the most. This horse trotted along, bent in the direction of travel, stretched through his topline, tracking up with his hind legs, nice and balanced and rhythmic. That ... was not Emma's experience with lunging. In fact, Ainsley had once told her to lunge as little as possible, just to "get the bucks out" because he was so unbalanced, and she would have better control to make him balance himself from the saddle.

This horse didn't need to be controlled to balance himself, and all at once it occurred to Emma, that this horse wasn't under "control" at all. He was doing exactly what they wanted him to, but there was absolutely nothing that could stop him if he didn't want to do it, the humans weren't even in the same space as him, he could run off to the far end of the arena and roll if he wanted to, and there was no way they could do any-thing about it.

It was amazing, really.

They were wrapping up this session and the student ducked under the barrier and walked over to where a halter hung on the arena fence, the horse following her at her shoulder like he was already wearing it, when the instructor said, "And re-member, for those who are brand new to this kind of training, that we just taught him to trot with no pressure whatsoever, and we could teach him to canter the same way. No chasing, no whips, nothing. Teaching speed without pressure means we aren't pushing them into fight or flight, we're not knocking them off balance, we're just setting it up so they choose to make the change in gait, at a moment when they are balanced and comfortable to do so, and all we have to do is tell them, 'yes, that's the right answer, here's a food reward'!"

No pressure at all. Emma was stunned. She wasn't sure she'd ever done anything with a horse that didn't use some kind of pressure. Pressure from her legs and heels and seat and crop and her hands all directed Thor every second. With no pressure, there was no way he'd do what she wanted, she was sure of it.

"Any questions while we give our horses time to switch?"

Emma had so many questions, but had no idea how to voice any of them, so she just kept scribbling in her notebook.

Teaching a trot with no pressure using a target and a reverse round pen. Pizza slices. Make the slices bigger. And she hoped she would remember what the heck that all meant.

Someone a few rows ahead of her raised their hand. "That was amazing, but what if we don't have the equipment to make a round pen like this?"

The instructor smiled as she answered. "You don't need a round pen like this one. Any round pen will work and a lot of it can even be done over any fence at all, a round pen works best for balance and means you can encourage forward motion and faster gaits without having to walk as far, but you can do quite a bit even with a straight fence."

"Yay!" Emma thought, *"I CAN teach Thunder stuff from out-side the fence!"*

Buy Feather Duster. Emma wrote in her notebook, then she switched to a red pen and surrounded it with stars.

The tall bay horse walked out of the arena at the side of his human, and a minute later another horse came in, very slowly and cautiously. This one was a beautiful dainty Arabian, a coppery chestnut with the dished face that proudly proclaimed her breed as soon as you saw her. She stopped dead and blew a loud snort when she spotted the pylons and poles of the round pen. She sounded just like Thunder, Emma thought in delight, and she leaned forward, pen poised so she wouldn't miss a thing.

"Tell me about her," the instructor asked, and the audience couldn't hear the answer so it was silent for a few moments while she listened to the owner of the beautiful chestnut mare.

"Is she more comfortable in her stall than this?" The instructor asked, watching the mare dance at the end of the lead, as she spooked four times in different directions at things that Emma couldn't identify, jostling her handler, until the handler gave a jerk on the lead, and the mare froze, but her head was high, and even at the distance Emma was at she could see the whites of her eyes as they rolled.

She was so scared, Emma thought, and wondered what they would do to help her. She had another twinge about Thor, and remembered bringing him into this same arena and his head high, eyes rolling. Had he been scared too? She hadn't helped him feel better if he had been. The clinician had told her to ride him forward and "get his attention" and she'd felt accomplished when he'd stopped spooking and jumped the pattern at last. But now she wondered ... had he been scared? Because making him do it anyway didn't seem like the right choice if he was scared. Even if that's what the experts had told her to do.

"All right," the instructor looked at the gathered auditors thoughtfully, "there's not too many people here, I think everyone will still be able to see. We're going to take poor Rosebud here back to her stall, where she's much more comfortable. In this environment she is so much over threshold that she's into her fight and flight. She can't learn anything in this state; we might get her to do something, but under this much stress she wouldn't retain it, so we'd be adding to her stress for absolutely no reason. But in a space where she's more comfortable, we will hopefully be able to get her back out of fight or flight, back into her para-sympathetic nervous system, and able to focus and learn. And if it goes well, we'll be able to give her the tools to make her more comfortable, the next time she's in a situation she finds stressful."

She sent the mare back out of the arena, and she spooked going through the gate, dragging her owner through behind her. *She is JUST like Thunder!* Emma was excited; this was just what she was hoping to learn about, she was sure now that she was going to be able to get some tools to help her teach Thunder to lead like a normal horse.

"We'll just give poor Rosebud a few moments to get safely back to her stall and chill out for a minute, and then if you'll go to the barn through the door on your left, and I'll meet you there to get you all to a spot you can see something without giving Rosebud heart failure."

There was a good natured chuckle from the assembled group of fifteen or twenty people, as they gathered their things and began making their way to the barn as instructed. Everyone was quiet and slow in their movements, in respect for Rosebud. Other horses in the barn were interested to see them, looking out of their stalls curiously. Emma recognised the bay horse from the previous session reaching out with his nose and happily getting some attention from the people as they passed.

The instructor had everyone stand in a semicircle around the stall, as far away as they could and still see, in order to minimize the stress on Rosebud.

"Also," she said, "we're going to work with Rosebud today in protective contact to make her more comfortable. For those who aren't familiar with that term, it simply means that we're going to have a barrier between us and our learner, our horse. It could be a fence in many cases but today we'll be using the stall door: Rosebud will be inside, we'll be outside."

Emma scrambled for her notebook and wrote: PROTECTIVE CONTACT = A FENCE. It was too hard switch to pens now that she was standing up, so she used capital letters instead of red stars to show importance. She suspected that "protective contact" was the term she'd needed when she'd tried to google the other night.

"Today we're going to start teaching Rosebud to touch a target. This is the perfect first skill to teach, because it's easy for them to learn, and sets up the method of communication we're going to use, teaching the horse that their behaviour is what earns the food reward, and that the click or whatever marker you've chosen, is a sign that the food reward is coming. So once again," clearly this was a review for most of the attendees, but Emma watched raptly, "we're going to show her the target, the moment she touches it with her nose – which most horses will because they naturally explore new things with their muzzle – then we click and reinforce." Emma was scribbling in her notebook without looking away, trying to both not miss anything, but also take detailed notes of everything that happened, "Now with a fearful horse, a target on a stick might be a problem, especially a horse who's been in a traditional training situation and associates sticks with whips and crops. We're going to start with Rosebud by shortening the handle, because our high tech feather duster target can do that." The group chuckled softly. "I think that will work for her, as she's not a feral horse, just a fearful one but in some cases, if we can't get them to engage with a hand held target we can start with a stationary target, something she can touch and we can reinforce without the human right there with it. I've used a cone as a stationary target, a plastic circle on the fence, and one mustang I worked with preferred a mat target as a first step, where he stood on it with his front feet, to a nose target. So there are lots of options, but I think this one will work for Rosebud." She turned to the stall and opened the headgate, so Rosebud could put her head right out if she was so inclined.

She wasn't.

"Up to this point, we've been using low value rewards of hay pellets with all our horses because we wanted motivation but also didn't want to lose the focus in the excitement of high value treats. In this case, we're going to use high value treats that we already know that Rosebud likes, as this is hard for her and we want her to feel motivated, but I am going to use some hay pellets in between if I can, because the extra chewing time might also be comforting for her."

She held out the treat, and Rosebud was able to take it without too much fuss.

"Aha," said the instructor, "proof of concept, now we can get started! You can see how much more settled she is in her own space right away. She's still pretty cautious, or maybe suspicious is a better word, but she's no longer over threshold."

Rosebud disappeared into her stall for a moment, then reappeared at the gate with a mouthful of hay.

"Yes, she's definitely feeling more comfortable, that's perfect if she'll go grab some hay whenever she wants it."

That surprised Emma. If you wanted her to earn a treat, didn't it make sense not to have other food available for her? Why would she do what they asked if she could just eat hay instead?

It was like she'd asked the question out loud, because the instructor answered it promptly. "We never want them to feel like they HAVE to do what we want in order to get the food. Especially a fearful horse like this, we would completely undermine her trust if she felt she had to do something that she wasn't really comfortable with, just to earn the food. Remember, food is a primary reinforcer, and highly motivating, another reason to usually go with lower value treats, to ensure your horse is truly comfortable, not just desperate because what you've offered is so delicious."

Emma wrote: *low value treats, available hay and chewing time is good.*

At least, she hoped she had, she still wasn't looking at the notebook while she wrote, not wanting to miss seeing anything.

The instructor held out the feather duster, on a very short handle, but kept it outside of Rosebud's stall, and the red mare made that dragon noise again but reached her muzzle out tentatively towards it.

The instructor clicked and gave Rosebud a treat. Emma was surprised, because she thought Rosebud was supposed to touch it to earn the food. Again, the question was answered for her.

"This is hard for Rosebud, so we never want to withhold the food, we want to reward every single effort, really any interaction with us at this point, to show her that this is a very rewarding activity and make her feel better about us humans and the silly things we do. She made a great effort, so I reinforced it." She held the target out again, and this time Rosebud reach out faster, without the dragon snort, but still stopped short of actually touching the feathers, though they moved with her breath as she sniffed it. Again, she got a food reward.

"I bet she touches it this time," said the instructor, "but I'm reminding myself that she doesn't have to. It's easy to get greedy trainer syndrome and wait too long, expect too much, and let her get discouraged. It's our job to make sure she always gets the right answer, and if she doesn't then we asked too much or didn't set her up properly. We never withhold the reward though, even if it doesn't work. Instead, we figure out how to ask the question differently next time."

Despite her words of warning, she would've won her bet. This time presented with a target, Rosebud stuck her nose out and touched the feathers, and the instructor clicked – using her tongue to make the sound, instead of a mechanical device – and then fed her a cookie, and a handful of pellets.

Soon, Rosebud had her head and neck completely out into the aisle, touching the target eagerly even when she had to lift her nose high or drop it down. The instructor was able to lengthen the handle and that made no difference.

"Now," she said, "let's do an experiment." She picked up the halter and entered the stall. Rosebud backed off cautiously at first, but soon returned happily to the target game. When she was settled and focused, she put on her halter, did a couple more targets, then slid the stall door wide open. The instructor walked out, holding the lead rope but giving the mare most of the lead, so there was no pressure on the halter at all. She put the target right at the doorway first. "Can you touch it here?" she asked, and Rosebud hesitated a moment, but then stepped up to touch it and earn her treat. A couple more repetitions, and then the instructor stepped back into the aisle and offered the target again.

Without being asked, Emma and all the other spectators shuffled out of the way to give her space, clearing the way back towards the arena.

Emma watched, in amazement, as the mare walked calmly and quietly, on a loose lead, from one offered target to the next, down the aisle and out into the arena. The spectators waited til she was in the ring, then returned to their seats as quietly as possible. No longer spread out in the bleachers, instead they all filed quickly into the front row to get sat down and not miss anything and avoid bothering Rosebud.

The instructor still had Rosebud on a very loose lead, draped in a big U shape, while she offered her the target, sometimes high, sometimes low, sometimes asking her to step forward to reach it. She addressed the audience, and even her voice on the loudspeaker didn't seem to bother Rosebud now she was focused on her new game.

"I want you to remember what you saw the first time Rosebud came in here. She was terrified, over threshold, trying to run away, unable to focus. She's still worried, we didn't fix that completely in this short time, but what we've done is given her something to focus on that is very rewarding and within her control. She touches the target, she gets a reward. It's comforting and consistent, and it keeps her in her parasympathetic nervous system, instead of the sympathetic system which is wired for survival. She can learn, she can understand that the arena isn't going to eat her. And we're at a place where she can start learning other things."

She smiled at Rosebud's owner and handed her the target and leadrope. "I think, though, that Rosebud has probably done enough for one day. Offer her a few more targets and one more exploratory loop, then slowly target your way out of here and back to her stall. Let's see if she can leave here with a bit less drama than she did last time."

Emma stifled a giggle remembering the poor owner popping through the arena gate after the horse, yanked along on the end of the leadrope and rubbed the mark left from her rope burn.

She couldn't wait to start introducing the target to Thunder.

She had learned so much! And there was still one more horse to go!

Chapter 12

Emma looked down at the funny slanted notes she'd taken while she was writing standing up, afraid to look down and miss anything, and started correcting a few words while she still remembered what she'd meant to write.

A lady with grey hair next to her chuckled. "I'm the same way," she said, "I write so fast I can't read my own writing!" she held up her own notebook, closed now.

Emma smiled at her. "This is so great, I don't want to miss anything!"

"It's a treat to see a youngster like you here," the lady said, "It took me forty years to learn there was a better way, I wish I'd started when I was your age." Emma thought her smile looked a little sad. "So many horses I've worked with who would have been so much better off." She sighed. "Oh well, we can only do the best we can with what we know, and the more we learn the better we can do." Her eyes darted to Emma's big supportive sling. "A horse accident?"

"Yep," Emma said. "We fell over a jump." Now it was her turn to sigh. "I wonder if it might not have happened at all if I'd learned about this way to work with horses before."

The grey haired lady put her hand on Emma's good arm for a moment. "We're all doing the best we can," she reiterated, "you can do better now that you know."

Emma nodded seriously. "I will," she said, and she meant it.

The gate opened and the final horse of the day entered the arena and if Emma had two good hands she would've clapped in delight and had to settle for bouncing in her seat. An audible "aww" came up from the other auditors around her.

It was a Miniature Horse, solid black, with as much hair as Thunder, but somehow even more unruly, so it nearly stood up around his head like a lion's mane. He practically bounced into the arena, and you could tell at a glance that he was the exact opposite of Rosebud; this little guy LOVED the arena and he looked over at the gathered audience, now all in the first row just on the other side of the fence from him, and tossed his head. Emma would've sworn it was for their benefit, and then he lifted his upper lip and lifted his nose in the air, showing his teeth in a big cheesy grin and getting a big laugh and a smattering of applause in return. Emma scrambled for her phone in case he did it again, she wanted a photo!

"He's a bit of a ham," his owner said, as the little black horse, clearly pleased with his first reaction, gave them another big smile and Emma took as many photos as she could, hoping one would work, as she knew that photos in arenas were sometimes tough to get focused.

The instructor was laughing as she asked, "Tell me about this little rockstar! And since we've got all our auditors in one place now, just come over here and they'll be able to hear too." They moved closer to the fence.

"I've done lots of trick training with him, using positive re-inforcement," said his owner, "and obviously he loves it, and has learned a lot, but he's gotten so pushy about the treats that sometimes I just have to put them away. I used to be able to let kids lead him and stuff, but now I don't trust him not to pick them up by the pockets and shake them in case treats fall out." Another round of laughter greeted this visual.

"What's his name?" The question came from the audience, not the clinician, but she nodded like it was a good one.

"Optimus Prime," This was met with more delighted laughter, and the owner raised her voice over it, "but we call him Opie mostly."

"Opie," said the instructor, "just needs to learn some food manners and that doing nothing is also a trick worth learning."

As she spoke, Opie demonstrated just what his owner had been talking about, and reached over and grabbed hold of the treat pouch with his teeth, while his owner tried to pry his teeth off and push him away. Emma thought of Thor, trying to stick his nose in her pocket after peppermints, and Ainsley standing between them to protect her.

"Let's turn him loose," the instructor jogged over to check the gate was latched, then indicated for the owner to take the halter off, "maybe he'll go exploring and give us a chance to chat first, and if not we'll go hide in the round pen on him."

But that wasn't necessary, as soon as the halter was removed Opie took off, racing around and bucking and putting on a great show for the delighted audience, and Emma switched her phone to video, because Mom and Granny had to see this.

"He's not used to being in a stall," his owner said, sounding both amused and apologetic. "Clearly there was some energy to use up."

"When we have a horse like Opie," the instructor said, as the pony in question found a great spot to roll and made a big show of it, circling and pawing and circling and pawing before he went down. "It's important to remember that instead of trying to get him to stop mugging for treats, we're focusing on something we'd like him to do INSTEAD of mugging for treats." She turned to the owner. "If he's not touching you with his nose, then he can't be grabbing the treat pouch, so that's the behaviour we want to make super reinforcing for him, muzzle not touching you."

Emma set her phone down, even though Opie was still being adorable, doing an air above the ground worthy of the Spanish

Riding School in Vienna, in order to grab her notebook and start writing.

For Thor – don't try to stop him from being pushy, instead reward him for something else. He can't be pushy if he's busy keeping his muzzle away.

"In some horses," the instructor was saying, "if they've really gotten dangerous, or are like Opie but 16 hands tall," *or 17 hands,* Emma thought of Thor again, "then we should really start this in protective contact. With Rosebud, we used protective contact and the "protective" part was for her, to make Rosebud feel safer from us. With a horse like Opie, we would be the one being protected, because we can easily step out of harms way of the teeth, and then reinforce the behaviour we want to see more of, without putting ourselves or our treat pouches in harms way."

Finished racing around investigating the arena, Opie was walking back looking intent.

"Oh lawd, he's comin'," the grey haired lady next to Emma quipped, and everyone laughed. Her comment seemed to give the instructor the giggles, and she had trouble stopping them before she could continue.

"I think, since Opie is so small, that I'm comfortable giving this a go without protective contact, but if any of you had the same sort of behaviour," this said as Opie walked around her in a teeny circle, leaning on her the whole way around and then made a grab for her treat pouch that she was just able to dodge, "even in a horse this small, I would definitely recommend the protective contact, and if you have a larger horse who is like this around food rewards," Opie made another loop, and this time she had to take a step to keep her balance, "then definitely don't try to work with them without a barrier. You can see why some people who don't know they need to start with those manners, say that food rewards create a dangerous horse. Because they can!"

She took a few steps and Opie followed. "Okay this isn't complicated, and since he already has some training and understands that his behaviour is what earns the treat, I suspect he's going to catch on to the basics," she looked over at his owner who had slipped through the gate into the bleachers, "though those basics are going to have to be reinforced continually for a while, because this is a pattern of behaviour that will take some time before it doesn't reoccur." The owner nodded.

"All right, so all I'm going to do for now is ignore him. I'm going to keep myself and my treat pouch safe, but otherwise I'm just waiting because when he realizes that I'm just standing here talking to you and not paying attention to what he's doing, he's going to look for something else to do, and the second that he does, I'm going to be ready." No sooner had she said it, than Opie, who had been nosing at and around her treat pouch and her hands, looked up at the audience, and the moment that his nose moved away from her, the instructor made the tongue click and fed him a treat.

"Notice," she said, "like we talked about this morning, I'm feeding him far away from my body, where I'd like his head to stay, not right at the pouch. Deliver the food where you'd like him to be."

Wait til he looks away, deliver food away from body. Emma wrote.

Opie finished his handful of hay pellets, and reached for another, nuzzling the pouch but suddenly he stopped, and pulled his nose away, facing the audience again. She clicked and fed him once more.

"Did you see his eyes looking sideways at me?" The instructor grinned, "Maybe you couldn't because of his excellent rockstar hair, but it's always my favourite part, when they look at me sideways like 'this is what you like?'"

Opie finished chewing and turned back towards the pouch but stopped before he even touched it and deliberately placed his head back forward, and he got clicked and treated and a little cheer from the audience.

"Now," the instructor said, "he's got the idea so this time I'm going to try to catch him before he reaches back toward me at all, and keep feeding him." As soon as he seemed to be close to finishing his mouthful, she clicked and fed him again, and repeated a few times, and Emma swore you could see him thinking, 'Wait I just have to *stand here* and she keeps feeding me?'

Finally, she let him finish and gave him a chance to make a choice and he looked at her, but didn't reach his nose over, and she clicked and fed him again.

"Now,' she said, giving him another handful, "with a horse like him that has a long history of mugging, it can be helpful to put this behaviour on a cue. Lots of people say 'manners' or 'be polite' or something like that, but of course it doesn't matter what word you choose, what do you think?"

"What about Bubble?" the owner suggested, "like, 'stay out of my'."

Everyone laughed again. "Great," said the instructor. "It should be pretty easy to add that cue every time you do it. He's going to make mistakes, just be consistent, feed lots, because chewing helps him chill and be still, feed far away from you, and he'll get better and better. He just thought that mugging was part of the process, and that if he didn't he wouldn't get his rewards. We have to break that superstition for him, and teach him that the food will come to him."

"Sometimes," the owner said, "he seems to get super excited about the food and tries to take it with his mouth wide open, like your whole hand is going to disappear down his gullet."

"Ah, yes!" The instructor said, "I'm surprised it hasn't come up before now, that's really common." She'd been clicking and feeding Opie while they talked, and he still stood happily, facing the audience. "Instead of offering the food normally when he gets like that, offer him the back of your fist first. He won't be able to get a hold of it, there won't be any food, and he'll automatically back off and close his mouth, then flip your hand over and let him take the food, and you'll get nice lips only instead of a gaping maw." She demonstrated the technique.

Offer back of fist if they are open mouthed taking food, then flip. Emma wrote.

The instructor had the owner come and walk around with Opie and then practice the same "bubble" game and it took only one try before he was just as good as he'd been for the instructor.

She was complimentary. "He's a very smart little man!" she said, "Of course I should expect nothing less from Optimus Prime!" Everyone laughed again and she continued, "I think we'd all love a demonstration of his tricks, if you'd be willing?" The auditors voiced their enthusiasm for that idea, and Emma scrambled to get her phone out again.

"Can you say hello to everyone, Opie?" she asked the little black horse, and he lifted a forelimb and pawed the air. Many of the auditors waved back to him, and Emma would've too if she'd had a free hand.

"Are you happy to be here?" she asked, pointing up in front of his nose and he gave them another big cheesy grin. She gave him a handful of pellets after every trick, and said to the instructor, "I'm remembering to feed him away from my body, and I think it's making a difference already!"

"Okay," she said to the audience, "here's his big money trick." She stood in front of Opie and said in a loud voice, "Autobots, Roll Out!" and threw her arms straight up over her head. Opie reared up on his hind legs and she walked backwards and he followed her, walking on his hind legs across nearly the whole width of the arena. The cheers grew as he went and by the time his front feet hit back on the dirt and they returned to the audience, the auditors had gotten to their feet in a teeny little standing ovation for the teeny little super star.

Facing the audience, both horse and handler took a bow, Opie going down on one knee into the dirt, and the cheers continued. Then with a cue that Emma missed (she'd have to rewatch the video), Opie laid down, then he sat up like a dog, and from the sitting position gave another cheesy grin.

The cheers continued, and Emma was blown away. She hadn't even considered that a horse could do so many fun tricks! She pressed stop on the video and held the phone to her chest. She was so happy she had that video, she could figure out how to do some of those tricks, she was sure of it.

When the cheers died down, it took only a moment, even with all the excitement, for Opie to remember his new skill of keeping his nose away. His owner was so pleased that she gave the instructor a hug. "I had no idea we'd be able to make this big a difference in one lesson," she said, "I know we'll have to keep it up and be consistent, but I'm just so pleased, it's going to be all fun again now, without all the frustration."

The grey haired lady next to Emma stood up then. "Let's give a big round of applause to our esteemed instructor!" she said, and when the enthusiastic clapping died down she added, "she has taught us so much today, and tirelessly answered our questions, and we are so grateful." She turned to the assembled group. "Shall we have her back again soon?" Cheers answered her and Emma did her best to clap using her one good hand against her knee. Imagine what she could learn if she could come for a whole day next time!

Emma was gathering her things to leave when she realized she hadn't even looked for the check in text Granny was going to send at 2 o'clock and here it was quarter to 4 and she scrambled for her phone. Sure enough, there was the text that said, "Hope you're having fun, let me know if you need anything! G ♥"

Emma frantically texted back. "Sorry I was so busy watching I didn't even notice the text or the time, sorry! All well, just finished."

She'd just hit send when she felt a gentle touch on her arm and turned to see Opie's owner smiling at her. "Oh!" Emma said, "I love Opie so much! I'm so glad I got to see him!"

The lady smiled at her. "I love him too, the clever little rascal. I noticed you were videoing him, would you mind sending that to me?"

"Of course not!" Emma handed her phone to her. "Put your number in and I'll send them all right away!"

It wasn't until after she'd done so, pushed send, and waved goodbye that she looked down and saw that the lady had put her number in under the name "Opie's mum" and that made Emma laugh.

Her phone buzzed in her hand and she saw a text from Granny that said, "Here" and she swung the shoulder strap of her bag over her head and nearly ran to the door, she was so excited to tell Granny all about it.

She crashed into the front seat so quickly that Granny looked up from her phone with a jump, clutching her chest.

"I'm sorry I didn't text you, but it was just so amazing, I didn't think of anything else I was just trying to learn and listen and write down as much as I could."

"I figured that was the case when I didn't hear from you, that's wonderful, I'm glad it was as good as you hoped! Sorry you weren't able to stay all day."

"That's okay, they said they might get her to come back again, and I left my number so they'll text me if she does." Emma danced in her seat. "I can't WAIT to try this stuff with Thunder!"

Granny turned out onto the road, then lifted one hand off the wheel to point at Emma. "You promised the doctor you were going to stay on the other side of the fence."

"Yes!" Emma said, "That's called 'protective contact' and not only will it keep me safe, but it will give Thunder more confidence because he knows he can walk away if he needs to, so he won't be so worried." She straightened abruptly and said, "Oh wait!" louder than she intended to.

Granny slowed the car and looked at her in alarm.

"Can we go to the dollar store?"

"You scared the life out of me." Granny said, "I thought I was going to hit something!"

"Sorry," Emma said sheepishly, "I got excited."

"What's exciting about the dollar store?"

"I need a feather duster."

Chapter 13

Emma leaped out of the car as soon as it had stopped, gathered her bag of supplies and went as fast as she dared to Thunder's paddock, speeding up when she realized he was at the far side and probably wouldn't be alarmed by her sudden approach.

She got the tub out and refilled it with the bag of treats they'd gotten at the tack store, and then pulled out her new target/duster she'd picked out at the dollar store, bought with the leftover cash she hadn't had to use for payment at the clinic. Hers wasn't feathers, but she thought that would probably be better. Instead, it had a microfibre covering with little nubbins on it to pick up the dust, but Emma thought it wouldn't blow in the wind like feathers would, which would be better for Thunder since she was working with him outside.

She'd picked a blue one to match his eyes.

By the time she was organized and looked up, her mom had caught up with her, and Thunder had come across the paddock to see what she was up to, standing just a short distance away from the fence and watching her. The barn door opened, and Ruby also came over.

"Good morning!" she said, "You're here early today, I've only just finished my chores!" She nodded at Thunder. "He sure remembers that you're his friend with the yummies!" Ruby noticed the duster in Emma's hand. "That's a new approach to grooming," she said, a twinkle in her eye.

Emma laughed and told her, "Actually, a new approach to training!"

"Really!" Ruby didn't laugh, she sounded intrigued. "Show me!"

"Well," Emma said, "I haven't tried it before, and he might be scared of the target, but I guess, let's try!"

"Can't do more than that!" Ruby said, and took a few steps away to go lean against the car, and Mom followed suit.

Start with where he's comfortable. Ruby remembered Rosebud and began by tossing a treat at his feet, which he picked up and then looked right at her while he chewed it. He was definitely paying attention, anyway! "Good boy!" she said, and then remembered the clicking sound she'd heard at the clinic, which she'd practiced all night.

She tossed another treat, a little closer and when he walked up to it and began to drop his head she clicked her tongue, and he paused, but didn't spook, just regarded her curiously for a moment before he picked up the treat. Hopefully that was helping him understand, but Emma didn't really know. She'd missed the bit about the clicker really, but she knew you used it the moment that the horse did something good.

The next treat she held out on the palm of her hand. "Come get it, what a clever boy you are," she began chattering away, and he didn't hesitate at all before walking up and taking the treat, surprising Emma so much that she was nearly late with her click, which once again made him pause, but didn't discourage him, as he took the treat and regarded her steadily while he chewed.

The next part was going to be trickier, since she could only use one arm. First, she picked up a treat, and held it in her left hand which was held tightly against her by the sling. Then she checked that the handle of the duster wasn't extended, and put it through the fence towards him.

"Can you touch the target, Thunder?" she said, knowing he didn't know what that meant at all, but that he seemed to like it when she chattered to him. "It's not scary, I promise, just check it out, and you'll see."

His nostrils flared, and he took a couple steps back, but there were no dragon noises, and he didn't run off, so Emma took that as a good sign. She lowered the target a bit, thinking it might be less scary if it was closer to the ground. She waited, and continued chattering to him, telling him about all the fun they could have with the target once he'd figured it out.

Finally, when she was just thinking she needed to find a new approach, he took a tentative step towards the target, and then another.

Reward the effort. Emma remembered. *Never withhold food.*

She balanced the target between her knee and the bottom of her sling, managing not to wiggle the end too much in the process, and tossed him a treat, which he ate eagerly, moving even closer to the target in the process of picking it up.

Emma restocked with easily reached treats while he chewed, stacking a row of them balanced along the top of her sling.

"That was great Thunder, you're so close. Aren't you curious what this thing is?" She wiggled the target ever so slightly to draw his attention to it, and he perked his ears, hooked his neck, gave a tiny version of his dragon snort, and reached out and touched it. Emma got her tongue click in just after he'd touched it – she hoped that was close enough – and managed to toss a treat quickly without bopping him with the target, which she was a bit afraid of while juggling everything.

She'd never missed the use of her left arm more, not at any time since the accident, but still. It worked. She'd done it. Thunder touched the target!

Before she'd even regrouped to ask for another attempt, Thunder looked at her for a moment then poked his nose out and deliberately touched the target with such a bump she felt it at the other end where it moved between her knee and sling. She clicked and tossed a treat.

And then he did it again.

And again.

She grinned over her shoulder at Mom and Ruby. This was going so well!

Time to move the target, she thought, trying to remember the steps they'd done with Rosebud yesterday.

She slowly lengthened the handle to give her a bit more reach, and Thunder touched it. She moved it to the left and he cheerfully took a step that direction to touch it again. To the right, no problem. She dropped it right to the ground, and he dropped his nose down to touch it. She lifted it high in the air, and he poked his nose up to reach it.

She wanted to stand up, see if he would follow her around the fence, but she remembered how they'd stopped Rosebud's session early, because they thought she'd learned enough for one day, and decided, very reluctantly, to be done. Ainsley had always told her to end on a good note when she was riding, and Emma really couldn't imagine a better good note to stop on.

Thunder had learned to touch a target! She'd taught him to touch a target!

She threw the remaining treats to him, then slowly stood up, walked away from the fence, and only then jumped up and down and indulged in a little shriek of joy.

"Did you see?" Emma ran over to her mom and hugged her. "He learned to touch a target, and he learned so fast!"

"I saw!" Her mom said, "And that means that you'll be able to start with the reverse pen thing you were telling me?"

"Yes! I can use it to teach him to lead without dragging, it will help him be confident with new things, he can learn tricks, all kinds of things! And now he understands that his behaviour is what earns the treat now, so that will make it much easier to teach him anything else too." She parroted the words she'd heard the day before, understanding them much better, now that she'd tried it for herself.

"Trailer loading," Ruby said thoughtfully. "I bet it would be great to help with teaching them to load in a trailer. Very interesting." She grinned at Emma. "Well done young lady! Come on into the kitchen, I think you've earned a treat too, I made a spice cake last night, would you like to help me eat it while you tell me all about all the rest of the sorcery you learned yesterday?"

Emma grinned, "Just let me get my notebook and my phone from the car – wait'll you see the little trick Miniature Horse that was there!"

***

When they got home, Emma asked her mom if they had a duster like the one they were using as a target, which they'd left at the farm.

"Why?" Mom sounded suspicious, "You want to do some dusting?"

Emma giggled, "No, I just want to practice handling it, to see if I can hold it in my hand in the sling." Her mom looked a bit alarmed and she hastened to add, "Just hold it, not move it!"

"Okay ..." Mom still seemed skeptical, but she went to the closet and returned after a bit of rummaging with a feather duster like the one they'd used at the clinic. It was pink. "Why do you want to hold it in your left hand?"

"I was thinking," Emma took the target – or duster, she guessed - and expanded the handle to it's longest, "that if I could hold it in my left hand then I could feed him the treat with my right, instead of throwing it for him. I think it would be good if he got used to taking it from me each time, and would help him get comfortable with me." She positioned the target with her right hand, then practiced passing it to her left, and mimed pulling a treat from her pocket and holding it out on the flat of her palm.

"Does it hurt your shoulder?" Her mom asked, looking at her sharply.

"No," Emma was pleased, "not at all, it's very light and my shoulder doesn't even notice." She looked around the room, "Now, where would I find something I could use as a fence to help me practice like it will be tomorrow?"

Mom looked around too. "What about the railing on the front step?"

Emma looked over. "Yes, that's pretty close, I'll go try, thanks Mom!" She took the duster and headed for the door.

"Maybe next you could use that duster for it's intended purpose." She called after Emma, but she was already out the door.

***

"Something wrong Em?" Emma's mom stopped on her way through the living room, and peered at her over the overfilled basket of laundry she carried. "You have a funny look on your face. Did you hurt your shoulder?"

"Oh, nothing like that," Emma tried to wave her hand dismissively, but the truth was she really was bothered, "I sent Ainsley the video of Opie doing his tricks because I thought she would like it."

Mom set the basket down on the couch and sat next to it, pulling out a towel and starting to fold it. "She didn't? I thought it was amazing!"

"No, she did, she liked it, but then she asked where it was. I told her at a positive reinforcement clinic at Green's."

"And?" Her mom prompted when Emma didn't continue, stacking the folded towel on the coffee table and reaching for another.

"And she said that she'd heard that was going on, sounded okay for silly tricks but you couldn't teach anything real with it." Emma sighed. "I was so excited about it, like it was a whole new way to communicate with horses, but maybe I was wrong."

Mom thought for a moment, still folding. "Do you think it's easier to teach 'silly tricks' than it is to teach serious stuff like jumping?"

Emma thought about it. "I don't know. I've never taught a trick. I don't think so? Some of those tricks Opie did I wouldn't have any idea how to start teaching them."

"I wouldn't worry too much about it. Even if she's right, and you can't use it for," Mom dropped a towel on her lap and made air quotes, "serious reasons, I watched you with Thunder, and the two of you were really communicating for the very first time." She finished the last towel, and started stacking them back into the basket.

"I guess," Emma still wasn't sure. Ainsley was her horse mentor, and had been for half her lifetime. If Ainsley thought it was silly, Emma thought it was probably silly.

Her mom bent over and kissed her forehead. "Stay excited Em. Even it if it is silly, you like it, and Thunder likes it, and I think you're probably the only two who really matter." She headed out of the room, but raised her voice so Emma could still here her while she was stacking towels in the closet. "Speaking of, I talked to Granny, and she is so excited to see this magic duster game of Thunder's that she postponed a meeting so she can take you to the farm for a demo first thing tomorrow!"

"That's great," Emma said, but she was having trouble getting back the same joy she'd felt this morning when she got home from the farm.

Emma had intended to review her notes again, to be sure she had it all fresh in her mind for the next day, when she was hoping she could start getting him to follow the target along the fence, which would be kinda like leading him, which seemed like a huge step from the horse who hated being led so much he kept dragging people around. It WOULD be a big step, she thought, and determinedly picked up her notebook, and a pen in case she wanted to jot any notes down for her plan for tomorrow. She'd just flipped the first page when her phone buzzed, and she took it out to read the message.

It was from Ainsley.

"I hope you aren't thinking of trying that treat training with Thunder. You don't want him getting mouthy or thinking he's the boss of you. Be safe."

Emma leaned back in the recliner and wished she could cross her arms.

Ainsley, who she trusted as a horse expert implicitly, told her that using food rewards was only for silly tricks, not real training, and would make horses mouthy and dangerous.

But the instructor who used food rewards all the time had said that horses just needed to know how to earn a treat, and she'd seen with her own eyes how quickly Opie had gone from mouthy and pushy to very polite and staying out of the human's bubble, USING treats.

It was very confusing, and she felt very deflated, like the excitement of yesterday's learning and this morning's progress with Thunder was soured, no longer as sweet and magical as it had seemed.

She sighed and put down the notebook. She needed a break from all of it, she thought, and turned on the TV instead.

Chapter 14

Despite Emma's determination to just stop thinking of it, Ainsley's comments had stewed in her brain, keeping her up half the night, but she had decided she wasn't changing her plans or approach. If it wasn't safe, that was okay, because Emma was in protective contact, so she couldn't get hurt anyway. If it was silly, then, so be it, she'd be silly. It wasn't like Thunder was off to a fancy horse show anytime soon, or maybe ever, so why was silly a bad thing?

It felt awkward though, not to listen to Ainsley after years of doing exactly as she taught her, and if Ainsley was right, that would be easier.

It would mean she could stop feeling badly about making Thor go over jumps with her spurs and her crop and her strength when he tried to duck out, making his dragon noise. She'd been thinking there must be a better way, using targets and food rewards to make him more comfortable jumping, but if not, then she hadn't done anything wrong. It if wasn't for Thunder, Emma realized, she would've just taken Ainsley's word for it, and dropped it.

If it wasn't for Thunder though, she never would've gone to the clinic in the first place.

No matter how weird it felt to disagree with Ainsley, Thunder deserved a fair chance to try this kind of training.

"You okay?" Granny looked over at her from the driver's seat, "You seem quiet, I thought you'd be bouncing off the walls after your big day teaching Thunder his first skill."

"Yeah. I'm fine," Emma said, deciding she didn't want to rehash it all again just now, "I didn't sleep very well is all, but I'm excited to show you Thunder's new trick!" And after she said it, Emma realized that it was true. She WAS excited, he'd caught on so quickly, what would they accomplish today?

Friends, she thought, remembering what Ruby had said the first night they'd brought him to her farm, *no matter what I'm doing or how I'm doing it, that's what I want. I want us to be friends.*

And no matter what Ainsley thinks, I believe this is the best way to do that. She raised her chin a bit, feeling resolved as they drove through the gate and passed the Cool Waters Miniature Horse Farm sign. *And Thunder is my horse, not Ainsley's, so its my decision.* She chuckled a bit to herself. *As long as I listen to the doctor and Mom and stay out of the pen, that is, then it's my decision.*

Granny parked, and after her pep talk to herself Emma felt a new surge of energy, and she leaped out, her notebook under her arm in case she wanted to refer to it. She went to the chair, pulled out the treat bin, and pulled the lid off. Inside was her neatly stored target, handle pushed in as far as it would go so that it would fit, and there was still plenty of treats. She pulled the target out, and before she could sit down, Thunder had trotted over, and stood near the fence watching her.

"Look at that," Granny spoke quietly from behind her. "I'm already impressed and you haven't even started! I can't believe he's already trotting *towards* a human like that."

Emma thought again of him on the first day she'd seen him, and remembered that it had been less than a week still, and paused for a moment to just look at him, standing so close she could nearly touch him if she stretched, and waiting calmly, bright blue eyes watching her as she tucked treats into her pocket and then more into her sling for easy access.

She should get a pouch like the one she'd seen them wearing at the clinic. She wondered if they made them with sparkles.

Emma still hadn't sat down, and Thunder didn't seem concerned by her standing, so she decided to start there. She extended the handle, and was about to stick it through the fence to ask him to touch it, when she remembered the clinician saying, Reward the Effort.

He'd made an effort trotting over to see her. He deserved a reward.

She tossed him a treat, and while he was eating it happily, she thought maybe she should've offered it on her hand, so she did that too, holding it flat out to him as far as she could reach.

It was a little different, with her standing, but Thunder hesitated only a moment before carefully picking it up. She didn't seem to have to worry about him trying to take it with a wide open mouth like they'd talked about at the clinic. He was very gentle, she only felt the faintest brush of his lips, no teeth at all.

"Good boy," she said to him, and she thought his ears moved at her voice, in a good way, not a scared way. "Are you ready to play the target game?"

He leaned back as she slid the target through the fence and into his space, but didn't take a step back and when she held it still and asked him, "Can you touch?" he regarded her without moving for a couple seconds, and then very deliberately poked his nose out and touched it. Emma made the tongue click sound, and, switching the handle of the target carefully to her slinged hand like she'd practiced, offered him a treat on her palm, mentally crossing her fingers. He took it. Emma watched him chew quietly, but inside she was leaping up and down celebrating.

Any doubt caused by Ainsley's comments had completely disappeared. This was so much fun, and Emma was convinced that Thunder was having fun too.

Using her new technique, she was able to adjust the position of the target with her good hand, hold it with the one in the sling, and deliver treats by hand. And she was getting smoother at it with repetition, and Thunder was too, getting very quick at touching as soon as she offered a new target position.

Emma withdrew the target from the fence. It was going so well, she was ready to experiment.

She walked a few steps along the fence, trying to move not slowly, but steadily, and Thunder reacted by backing away, but he didn't spin and run, so Emma took that as a good sign and confidently offered the target through the fence again. "Can you touch the target, Thunder?" She tried to keep her voice as nonchalant as she could, not like she wanted this more than anything. Emma just had time to think, *oh no, it's not going to work* when he dropped his head and walked up just as confidently as ever to touch the target and earn his treat. "Good boy!" Emma cheered him on, "You are the smartest and prettiest boy ever!"

She moved again, and again, and every time he waited where he was, sometimes backing a step or two, sometimes not, but always eagerly walking to touch the target when she offered it. "Are you watching, Granny? Can you believe it?"

"I can't believe it!" Granny's voice came from behind her, closer than Emma expected, and she looked over her shoulder to see her following along with her phone out. "I had to get a video so your mom would believe it!"

Emma went to move along the fence again, and this time, instead of waiting, Thunder walked when she did, and was ready and waiting when she offered him the target again.

Before long, they were walking side by side, Emma outside the fence, and Thunder inside. When she stopped, he stopped, and she'd give him a treat, and then when she stepped off, he would too, right in step with her and walked happily along until she stopped again to give him another treat. Then she had a thought and changed directions, to see if he'd still come, and he turned as quick as she did to fall in beside her again. She fed him and looked up to see Ruby standing in the middle of the yard watching.

"Amazing!" Ruby said, "I never would've believed it that you'd be working together like that already!"

"Me neither!" Emma fed him another treat, and realized she was nearly out, so gave him all she had left in a pile on the ground and walked away from the fence while he was eating.

Once she was at a safe distance she squealed and bounced, and Granny met her with a bear hug.

"I have never seen anything like that!" Granny squeezed her as tight as the sling would allow. "I got it on video, I'll send it to your mom right away, she'll be so proud!"

Emma looked over at Thunder, who still watched her from the spot on the fence where she'd left him. "I'd like to keep playing, but Ainsley says you should quit when it's going really well, and," she giggled, "It's going REALLY well!"

"I'll say," Ruby said, "I wish I'd known about a magic duster decades ago, it's a game changer!"

"I wonder if I can run a bit, with my shoulder." Emma didn't wait for them to weigh in, and gave it a try, gently jogging slowly across the yard. "Yeah that's okay I think, the sling holds it strong, as long as I'm careful." She looked over at Thunder. "Tomorrow we'll try a little trot!" She called to him, and he still stood and listened to her.

"Very little," Granny was trying to sound firm, Emma recognized the tone, "If you fell, you'd really do yourself in, and have a whole new injury and surgery to recover from."

Ruby leaned over conspiratorially. "The side closest to the barn is the smoothest, less chance of tripping."

Emma made the decision quickly, in no small part because she was afraid that her mom would give the plan a firm NO if she heard about it, and went and refilled her pocket with treats. Thunder walked over quickly to meet her and she showed him the target and started the process again. Touch-click-treat-walk, repeat until they got to the side that Ruby had said was safest.

"I'm videoing so you can see it," Granny called, "You watch your own feet, and I'll watch Thunder."

Emma gave a thumbs up; that was probably a good idea. She could definitely see herself getting so distracted watching to see if he was trotting that she would trip over her own feet.

She started walking and he was right with her, and when she got nice and straight she said, "Come on, Thunder!" and started to jog. She looked resolutely at her own feet, and moved carefully and steadily. She didn't look, but she was sure he wasn't coming and felt a stab of disappointment. *Aw well,* she thought, *he's already done amazing today,* and then she heard the sound of his hoof beats and his head came into view in her peripheral vision.

He was doing it! They were trotting! Emma clicked her tongue, stopped and fed him a treat, and then another, and then another. "You are magic," she told him, "Magic Thunder, that's your name." Without thinking, after he took the last treat she reached up and rubbed his forehead, under that thick white forelock, and she was already doing it before she realized that was the first time she'd ever touched him, and her eyes filled with tears. "Magic Thunder," she whispered to him, "thank you for finding me." She fed him every treat she had, then rubbed his face once more and stepped away.

She looked at the dollar store extendable microfiber duster that she held in her hand, now a bit grubby from Thunder's nose and dusty from storing in the treat bin. She held it up to show Granny and Ruby. "This isn't a duster. It's not a target either. It's a magic wand!"

***

Emma was curled up in the recliner, wrapped up in a fuzzy blanket, with a cup of hot chocolate balanced precariously on the arm. She was supposed to be watching the new episode of Doctor Who with her mom, but she was actually watching and rewatching the video that Granny had sent her on her phone. She never got tired of it, it was almost as magical to watch it as it had been to live it. He'd trotted with her! With no halter or lead and not even on the same side of the fence! She looked at the faint shiny spot on her palm, where he'd yanked the lead rope out of her hand the day she'd first met him. That was only six days ago. How was that possible! She slid the video along to where she'd reached over and rubbed his forehead, then paused and took a screenshot.

Granny had gotten a great angle. All that practice getting photos of houses meant she was really good with a camera phone, and the screenshot was a beautiful photo. Emma touched the share button and posted it on her Instagram stories, with a gif of the word MAGIC sparkling across it.

She almost sent the video to Ainsley. That's what she would normally have done with a fun horse video, or really any videos of Thor doing anything. She even had it ready to send, but then cancelled it.

Today was magical, completely magical, and she was afraid that Ainsley wouldn't understand, and would say something to ruin it for her again.

Emma wanted to keep this feeling of excitement and success and magic as long as she could. Even if that meant keeping it to herself.

Her mom laughed delightedly at something the Doctor said on TV, and Emma tried to pay attention to the show, but thirty seconds later she unlocked her phone again, and watched the video one more time.

Magic Thunder was even more exciting than the TARDIS and all of time and space.

Chapter 15

Emma was eating her breakfast the next morning, when her phone buzzed. She reached for it eagerly, hoping it was Granny; she'd promised to text and let her know when she could squeeze in a short visit with Thunder today.

But it wasn't Granny, it was Ainsley, and Emma felt a little jolt of worry in her stomach when she saw her name.

How odd, she thought, when she used to be one of her favourite names to see on her phone.

Ainsley had replied to her instagram story about Thunder. The notification only showed the first few words and Emma read "ainsleystoneridge replied to your story: "So cute! He's not nearly ..." and she clicked on it to read the rest with surprising trepidation.

"He's not nearly as wild as they said he was!"

Emma frowned. But she wasn't sure why. It wasn't a bad comment, but she didn't think it was accurate really. He was just as wild as they thought he was, but the new techniques Emma had learned had given him confidence.

Right? She was second guessing again, and Ainsley hadn't even said anything against what she was doing.

Of course, Ainsley didn't know what Emma was doing.

Emma was still staring at the Instagram comment, when a new message popped up, this time a text message from Ainsley.

"Will you come see Thor again soon? I think he misses you! Vet appointment yesterday, they started the new stem cell therapy, might see improvement as soon as tomorrow. ◈◈ Will recheck ultrasound next week, then we'll know more."

Emma paused for a minute, then replied. "Will try to come soon, crossing my fingers the stem cells help! Give him a peppermint from me! ♥♥♥"

Nothing about Thunder. Or the clinic. Good. Safe.

"I hear you're having fun with Thunder! Send me a video please, I wanna see!"

Emma's stomach dropped, but she couldn't very well say "No" without explaining that she thought Ainsley was out to lunch with her opinions on food rewards and she was definitely not going to do that, so she waited until after she'd finished her breakfast, brushed her teeth, and got dressed before she sent the video, in the hopes that Ainsley would be busy by then and not have time to watch it right away. She just sent the last one, where he trotted with her and she petted his face, and she trimmed it first so Ainsley wouldn't see how many treats she'd given him at the end, since she hoped that would avoid a conversation about spoiling him, because Emma was pretty sure he'd earned those treats and didn't want to have to disagree with Ainsley.

She'd just set the phone down when it buzzed again and she picked it up gingerly, worried about what she might read and wondering at how fast Ainsley had watched the video and responded, but it was Granny, so Emma opened the text eagerly.

"Can pick you up for a SHORT visit at 11:30, and if we're careful should have time to stop for McNuggets after. See you then! Can't wait to see what you and Thunder will do today!"

Yay! Emma thought, and with an effort pushed any worries about what Ainsley would say about the video out of her mind.

She went and got her notebook. Her mom had suggested adding a training journal to it, and she had written all about her previous sessions with him, and she scanned over them, then wrote today's date, then PLAN in big letters with two underlines.

Review target, following, turning. Probably not trotting. Emma thought she'd pushed her luck enough on that one, she'd wait for the okay from the doctor to do it again.)

Ideas for other through the fence activities: petting further back along his body, maybe brushing? Would be fun to brush his mane!

Tricks???

She put three question marks after tricks, because she didn't really know how to teach any, though it seemed like she should be able to from the other side of the fence. She pulled up the video of little Opie, which even though it was delightful didn't really give her a place to start.

Next, she tried YouTube and searched trick training but she didn't like the first video she saw, where a girl was using a rope around a horse's leg to get them to lie down. Quickly she backed out of that one and searched again. "positive reinforcement trick training using a target" – that was better, no more ropes. A girl who didn't look any older than Emma was using a long handled target to get her horse to spin in a small circle. That looked promising!

Emma added "spin" to her notebook and then leaped up to get ready. It was almost an hour until Granny would be there to get her, but Emma wanted to be completely ready and waiting on the step so they wouldn't waste a second of their Thunder time.

"I know the doctor was emphatic about you staying outside the fence," Granny said while they made the short drive to the farm, "but I think if you explain that you're not attached to the horse and that he is tiny, you might get the okay to work with him inside the fence at your next appointment. Don't you think he would be just as good for you if you were in there?"

"I don't know," Emma said. "He might be much more scared because he might think I could grab him and make him put on a halter, but I'd sure like to try it!" She bounced a bit in her seat at the idea. "Once the doctor gives me the okay though, we'll have more time spent together like this, and maybe that's a good thing, and Thunder will trust me more when I do get in there." She frowned as a sudden thought struck her. "I think he's very worried about the halter though, I bet I could start getting him used to it from the outside of the fence too. I read something online about using the halter as a target." She pulled out her notebook and wrote *target the halter*, just as they pulled into the yard.

"What are you going to start with?" Granny asked as they got out of the car.

"Review!" Emma said, "Same as yesterday, but I'm not going to run this time."

"Ah yeah, your mother gave me heck for that too." Granny winked at her, "I think it was worth it though."

Emma laughed as she got her target out, and then looked up to greet Thunder who was trotting across the pen towards her. Trotting! "Good morning, Thunder!" She called to him and held out a treat for him as soon as he arrived – trotting towards her was *definitely* something she wanted to reinforce so it would happen again!

She carried her target, but he seemed to be following her body so she didn't offer it to him as she walked the perimeter of the fence, stopping at irregular intervals to feed him, and he kept pace with her beautifully. Emma had the thought that he "led" better without a halter than most horses did with one.

"Okay then," she said to him, "if you're so clever let's try this." And she switched direction quickly, to see if she could get away on him, but he wheeled and caught up, so she switched again and so did he and she laughed and gave him a treat. He seemed to have a sparkle in his eye, like he enjoyed the game too, so she tried hopping back and forth quickly, but that was too much for him and he just backed up, his head high staring at her, and she apologized. "Okay, too much, my bad." She offered him the target and he walked up, touched it with his nose, got his treat, and all was forgiven.

"Let's try something new then," Emma said, making sure the target handle was as long as it would go. She reached over the fence with it, and once he'd touched it and been reinforced a couple times in the new position, she said, "Can you follow it?" and started moving it towards his hip. He stretched his neck around at first, but then stepped his hind end over and turned away from her to touch it. Emma clicked her tongue, and he came back to her to get his treat. "That was great!" she told him, "first step of spin!"

It took a few minutes to coordinate her positioning, standing on her tip toes to get the target over the fence and where she wanted it, and his understanding of what the heck the target was doing now, but Emma kept hearing the positive reinforcement instructor saying "never withhold the food, reward the effort" so she just kept giving him a treat and trying again, and all of a sudden it worked, and they both looked at each other in surprise as he'd found his way back around to face her again after following his target in a neat little circle. Emma hurried to click and fed him a whole handful of treats, raving about what a clever boy he was while he chewed. When he was finished, she said, "Can we try it again? Spin!" and positioned her target, and this time he seemed to have figured out the coordination and had no trouble making his little circle.

Oh, this was fun! Once he was good at it, and could do it without the target, maybe she could spin at the same time and it would be like they were dancing! Emma remembered seeing a competition at a dog show where it was like they were dancing with their dogs and doing all kinds of tricks together, if there wasn't something like that for horses, then there should be, that would be so much fun!

"Did you get a video, Granny?" she called over her shoulder.

"You betcha! You're going to have him dancing next!"

Emma laughed, "You just read my mind, I was thinking the very same thing!" Her mind was racing now. What else could she teach him? What would he really love to do? She thought of everything she knew about him, and remembered the way he sailed over the fence. "I'll be right back," she told him, tossing a treat on the ground for him to find to keep him busy while she hurried over to the barn.

"Where are you going?" Granny called after her.

"I have an idea, I'll be right back!"

Granny looked down at her phone, "Hey Em, I have a call I have to take, I'll just be in the car, okay?"

"Okay!" Emma ducked into the barn and looked around her. Hung in neat rows on the end were manure forks (with narrow tines for miniature poop, Emma needed to find one of those now she had a miniature poop maker!) and brooms, and Emma grabbed a broom, choosing the most 'well used' one, it's bristles worn down to stubs, and headed back outside.

She could see Granny inside the car across the yard, talking animatedly, and Emma knew it must be a real estate client she was talking to, she had her sales face on. Emma headed to the closest side of Thunder's pen, where Ruby had said it was the flattest ground. She stuck the broom handle through the fence, so it was about knee height where the broom itself stuck out, and then angled towards the ground, and then she walked back to the corner and called Thunder.

"Magic Thunder, can you come touch the target?" She held it out to him and once again he trotted across to touch it. She wished she'd thought to get her phone out and video that. It just warmed her heart to see him trotting towards her like that, ears up and eyes bright, and she would love to have that to watch over and over during the long hours when she wasn't here with him. As she fed him a treat she made a mental note to call him again before she left and try and get the video.

"Okay, Thunder, do you see that broom handle sticking into the pen there?" She pointed, chattering to him even though she knew he didn't know what she was saying, "That's not a broom handle, it's a jump! Just for you! Did you want to try?"

Emma walked quickly along the fence, lengthening her stride but not running, and looked sideways to see what he would do when he got to the broom, hoping to see him soaring over it, his mane flying through the air majestically.

Instead, he shied and looped out around it and then came back to the fence and looked at her. Emma laughed and gave him a treat.

"Okay, fail." Emma rubbed his forehead while she thought. "Let's try again, did you want to go look at it first?" She walked over to the broom and he came with her, but cautiously, dropping his head, then lifting it again to look at the suspicious item that had appeared in his pen. "It's safe, I promise," Emma said, reaching through and putting her hand on it, then she had an idea. "Can you touch?" she asked and Thunder blinked at her for a minute, then reached down and touched the end of the broom handle just as he would've the duster. Immediately he began to explore it, running his nose along the wood and sniffing loudly. "See!" Emma felt triumphant, "I told you! It's just like a target, now come on!"

She headed back to the corner to start again, a bit worried that she'd now taught him to stop and put his nose on it, but that would be hilarious, if not what she was going for, so really, no downside.

Once again, she started down the fence as fast as she could go without running or risking a fall, and Thunder kept pace with her, not quite trotting but striding right out at his walk, and when she got to the broom she turned to look at Thunder and he stopped and turned to look at her.

"Oh," Emma said, as all the times that Ainsley had hollered across the arena at her to 'look where you're going not at the jump' flashed into her mind. "That was definitely my fault Thunder, you did just what I did, I'll do better next time." And she gave him a treat because even if he didn't do what she wanted he'd made an effort and deserved his reward.

Third times the charm, Emma thought, or hoped, as they reset back at the corner again. This time Emma focused all her attention on the corner at the end of the paddock, and walked towards it with as much purpose and intent as she could, just as when she was trying to keep Thor straight down a line of jumps. She tried to see Thunder out of her peripheral vision, but was careful not to change her focus or turn her head or slow her pace as she got to the broom, and just as she worried she wouldn't be able to tell if he'd jumped it or not he was suddenly way up in the air by her shoulder and then he landed and galloped off ahead of her, tossing his head from side to side. She clicked her tongue, and laughed delightedly as he circled back to her and she gave him treat after treat.

"You DO love to jump!" she told him, as she rubbed his face. "That was amazing, we'll figure out more jumps for you, I promise!"

A car door slammed and Emma looked up eagerly, hoping it meant that Granny was done with her call and could video his next jump attempt, and that the same adorable celebration would happen again.

Ainsley's truck was over by the gate, and Ainsley herself was coming across the yard. Emma didn't know how to feel, and wished she didn't have the target in her hand still.

"Hey!" Ainsley waved cheerfully. "I had a lesson cancel last minute, so I thought I'd pop up and see the little big man – I pulled in just as he went over that jump, that was amazing!"

Emma relaxed a little. This seemed like once again she and Ainsley were on the same page. That was good. "Did you see how happy he was? Can you video him?" Emma handed her phone over. "I want to try it one more time, make sure it wasn't a fluke!"

"Yes, hang on, let me get a good angle," Ainsley jogged over toward the corner of the barn and Emma turned back to Thunder's fence again.

"Come on Thunder!" Emma held out the target and he trotted over, touched it, and got his treat, then she started down the fence again, trying not to be nervous with a new audience member, and hoping that her nerves wouldn't throw him off.

If they did, his love of jumping overcame them, because before she'd gotten to the jump he'd picked up speed and passed her, sailing over the little broom handle, about twice as high as he needed to jump to clear it, and then once again tossing his head, even giving one big buck before coming around in a big circle to meet her and get his treat. Emma had a great view and she loved it.

"He loves that so much!" Ainsley's delighted voice came from behind her as she jogged up to show Emma the video she'd taken. "That's so cool that he's doing it on the other side of the fence!"

Emma felt so much relief that Ainsley thought so too. She had been worried she would say it was silly again, or that the treats were bad. "Are you going to do it again? I can video more if you want?"

Emma shook her head. "I'd love to, but you always say to quit when it's going good, and that was very good."

"It was very good, and good for you for doing what I say and not what I do! I should take my own advice." Emma thought Ainsley looked a little troubled, but her face cleared quickly. "Then what are you going to do next?"

"I thought I might see if he'd let me brush his mane," she said, "It's so pretty, I've been itching to get a comb in it."

"I could catch him for you!" Ainsley said eagerly, "And then we could give him a proper grooming." She looked over at the catch pen. "If I can get him in the panels I can get a halter on him, and then he won't have a choice but to put up with us."

Her words were light, but Emma didn't like the sound of them. She was sure that she'd made so much progress with Thunder already because he DID have a choice. She had wanted to get him used to a halter slowly, from outside the fence first. Ainsley was looking at her expectantly, waiting for her response.

"I don't think we have time for all that," she said, her voice sounding a bit shaky to her own ears, "Granny has a meeting soon, I was just going to reach through the fence, he's letting me pet his face and neck now, so hopefully he'll ...." Her voice trailed off as Ainsley talked over her.

"It won't take long! I'm a good tiny horse catcher, I have lots of experience!" She turned towards the barn. "I'll get a halter!"

"I'm not supposed to be on the same side of the fence as him, the doctor said," Emma was starting to feel desperate.

"That's okay, I'll catch him, and you can brush through the fence or something, we'll figure out how to do it safely for you." Ainsley was almost to the barn.

What about safely for Thunder? Emma thought and as Ainsley opened the barn door she steeled herself and said, "I don't want you to catch him."

It had taken so much nerve to say it, that it had come out a lot louder than she'd intended, and her cheeks burned with embarrassment.

Ainsley turned to look at her. "What?" she looked confused, and maybe a little hurt. "Why?"

Emma's words tumbled over themselves as she tried to explain. "I don't think he's ready, we're making friends through protective contact to give him confidence, and if we corner him and catch him I'm afraid that he won't want to play with me anymore."

Ainsley scoffed. "So, you're just never going to put a halter on him in order to be his friend? How are you going to trim his feet? Or groom him, or anything else? He's just going to live in that pen the rest of his life?"

"No!" Emma said, "I will get him back on the halter, but not yet, once he's more comfortable with me in his space, and has gotten used to the halter. I don't want him to think that halters are just for dragging him around, or for him to drag people around."

"You think he could drag me around?" Now Ainsley definitely sounded annoyed. "I think I can handle him."

"I know you can!" Emma said pleadingly, "But I don't think it's good for him."

"I see," Ainsley crossed her arms over her chest. "You went to one hippy dippy clinic and now you think that you know more than me and I'm doing everything wrong."

"No!" Emma felt tears prick at the back of her eyes, "That's not it at all, it's just that Thunder ..."

"What's going on?" Granny walked over, putting her phone in her pocket and looking from Emma to Ainsley and back again with concern on her face.

"It's nothing," Ainsley said, "Emma just wants to do things her way, and that's fine, he's her horse." She looked at her watch. "Well, look at the time, I gotta get back to work anyway." She handed Emma her phone back, stalked to her truck and left, while Emma just stood there, feeling lost, and the tears that had been threatening overflowed.

Granny was there in an instant, folding Emma in her arms and patting and soothing her as she sobbed. "What on earth happened?" she sounded mystified. "It looked like you were having so much fun, I saw Thunder jump that broom like crazy, and I thought Ainsley would love it!"

Emma felt a fresh round of sobs rise in her throat and tried to swallow them, mostly successfully. "I was, he did, she did." With a shaky breath, Emma held herself away from Granny's support and wiped her eyes. "She wanted to go get a halter and put him in the catch pen and tie him up so we could groom him. I didn't think that was a good idea, I thought he wasn't ready and he wouldn't want to play anymore. I told her no." Emma's face crumpled again at the memory. "And now she thinks I don't trust her, and that I think I know better than she does, and she hates me."

The last words came out in a wail despite her best efforts and Granny folded her in her arms, patting her head and shushing her. "Don't be silly," she said, but it was soothing, not dismissive, "she doesn't hate you, she's just getting used to the idea that you're not a little girl anymore who does whatever she says. Now you listen to me," Granny pulled back and lifted Emma's chin to make her look at her. "I am very proud of you."

Emma was confused. "Why?"

"That little horse over there," Granny gestured with her head, and Emma looked over to see Thunder still standing at the fence, watching them curiously, "relies on you to make decisions that are in his best interest, and today you said no to someone you love and respect, because you didn't think it was right for him. I know how hard that was for you, and you did it. You did what you thought was right, you spoke up for Thunder." She put her forehead against Emma's. "You are a brave girl, and you should be proud of yourself, too."

Emma thought about that. She was so sad that Ainsley had left in a huff, and she was afraid that was the end of it – that she would never get to learn anything else from her, that she wouldn't get to go see Thor, that it was all over.

But Granny was right, she was relieved too, that Ainsley had listened to her, and hadn't chased Thunder into that pen, and put the halter on him, and won a tug of war with him to make him behave. Because she remembered how Thunder behaved after that, but with his head down, not even looking around, like he was a different horse than the bright and engaged one who played with her across the fence. She knew, with a certainty she felt to her bones, that she'd made the right choice for Thunder, and that was the most important thing.

"You're right, Granny." Emma straightened her shoulders. "Hopefully I can find a way to explain it to Ainsley so she can understand why I said no, but I can never explain to Thunder if I let something scary happen to him that he wasn't ready for. I protected him."

"You did, and now I think you better go visit with him, he looks worried about you."

Emma giggled a little, because that was silly, but it did seem like she could see concern in his blue eyes and when she crouched near him at the other side of the fence he stuck his nose through and lipped at her sleeve. "You are the goodest boy," she told him, "And keeping you safe and happy is worth it." Emma reached through and scratched behind his ear, and he made funny faces, his lip working as though he was scratching too.

"There," Granny said behind her with satisfaction. "Now you both feel better."

"I guess we do," Emma sighed, "We're probably late, hey Granny?"

She looked at her phone. "I think you have time for one more jump if you wanted, and then you'll have to hurry and put that broom away and say your goodbyes to Thunder if we're going to have time for lunch before I have to head back to work."

"What do you think?" Emma said to Thunder, "One more jump?" She got to her feet and headed for the corner, and he trotted after her eagerly.

"Wait, wait, wait," Granny called, and Emma stopped, looking over. "I need to get my phone out and looks like Ruby's just pulling in, she'll want to see too, just wait one minute!" Emma crouched down and went back to scratching Thunder, working her way down to his chest, which he seemed to love, as he stuck his wiggly nose through the wire and rubbed the top of her head.

"Aw," Emma said, "Are you scratching me back, that's so sweet!"

"Okay!" Granny called, "we're ready whenever you are!" and Emma looked over to see both Granny and Ruby ready with cell phones pointed at her and she grinned. Her own private videographers.

"Are you ready for a jump?" Emma got to her feet and said, "let's go!" as she started walking with long strides in the direction of the broom.

Thunder took off ahead of her right away this time, cantering towards the tiny makeshift jump, clearing it easily, and then doing his happy bucking head shaking routine, tossing his mane as he looped around and cantered up to Emma, where she stood watching him in awe. "That was amazing!" she told him, digging out all the cookies she had left and holding them out to him in a double handful that he dove into, as many falling on the ground for him to clean up later as he managed to cram into his mouth.

Granny and Ruby both clapped enthusiastically as she walked back to them and she grinned, still feeling a little down but how could she be too sad with such an amazing little horse learning such cool things and having so much fun.

"You know," Emma said, as a thought occurred to her, "if I hadn't run into Thunder that day, I'd still be stuck on that recliner moping and waiting to heal, instead of having all this fun."

She hugged her Granny. "Thank you for making him mine."

Then she hugged Ruby. "Thank you for letting him live here."

***

Emma was full of mixed emotions when her mom got home and she told her all about her day.

"I'm so happy about Thunder and all the fun we're having, and I can't wait to try the next thing. Ruby says she has lots of jumps and obstacles we can play with, and she'll help me set them up around the fence so we can work on them with me still safely outside. That's all so exciting, but I'm so sad about Ainsley, and I don't know how to explain to her that I'm so grateful for everything she's taught me, and that I DO trust her, I just had to make the choice I thought was best for Thunder."

Her mom, sat down across the kitchen table, and reached across to put her hand on Emma's arm. "Why don't you tell her that? Just send her a text and say just that: 'I'm so grateful for everything you've taught me, I wouldn't have had a clue how to deal with Thunder without it, I'm sorry if I hurt your feelings but I just had to make the decision I thought was best for him in that moment.'"

Emma shuddered at the idea. "I'm sure you're right, but I don't think I'm ready to do that. What if she gets mad at me again?"

Mom squeezed her arm. "I don't think it'll get easier if you wait, it might even get worse."

Emma groaned. "I guess if I do it now then I've done something and can stop thinking about it all the time. Hopefully." She grabbed her phone, typed the message, and sent it before she could think about it too long. "Now I'm putting it on airplane mode," she declared, "Because then I can at least put off dealing with her response – or lack of response."

Her mom laughed. "That's fair, it'll keep til morning! Now show me the video of him jumping again!"

Chapter 16

Emma was eating breakfast with her mom before she left for work the next morning when she turned the notifications back on for her phone, with great trepidation. In fact, she might've just left them off for the day, but didn't want to miss Granny's texts, and kinda wanted to share the video Granny had sent of Thunder's last jump on her Insta.

Sure enough, it promptly started buzzing and Emma peeked at it, making a face like she thought a spider might jump out of the phone screen.

Sure enough, it was from Ainsley. "Don't worry about it Emma, you have every right to make the decisions you want for your horse, I shouldn't have pushed you on it. But just remember, we can't let our full sized horses do whatever they want like you can with Thunder, we have to use tools other than cookies and dusters with them."

Emma frowned.

"Uh oh," said her mom, setting her coffee cup down, "What did Ainsley say now?" Emma slid her phone over to her. "Well that's not so bad!" Mom said, "She doesn't sound mad at you at all!"

"No, but it doesn't make sense," Emma said. "There were horses of all sizes at the clinic, and they treated them exactly the same. The first horse was nearly as tall as Thor, and they used a target and treats and he did all kinds of things, and was calm and happy to do it. And then Rosebud, she was an

Arabian and she was so scared of the arena, and then they taught her the target and it helped her not be scared anymore. Why would it be any different because the horse is bigger or smaller?"

"You're asking the wrong person, sorry, Em." Mom got up and dropped a kiss on top of her head. "Why don't you do some research online today and see if you can figure out if there's actually a difference?" She picked up her jacket off a nearby chair and slid it on. "And keep in mind, Ainsley can be right about a lot of things about horses and wrong about this. It's not her fault, she just hasn't had a chance to learn it yet, give her the benefit of the doubt, maybe this time you can teach her something cool instead of the other way around."

Emma thought about that for a long time after Mom had left for work. But how could she teach Ainsley something that she wasn't interested in learning?

She looked on YouTube, and found so many videos of horses, of every size, learning all sorts of skills using targets and food rewards. There was an amazing video of a horse – a full sized horse - who had been dangerous to give needles to, and now stood with not even a halter on and touched a target to give the vet permission to give him his needle. It looked like magic, but after she was able to teach Thunder to jump by remote control on the other side of a fence, Emma believed wholeheartedly in this sort of magic.

When she got thirsty and stopped watching videos to go get a glass of water (being responsible instead of getting the root beer she really wanted) she was completely convinced.

Ainsley was wrong.

Targets and treats and giving horse's choices was good for any size of horse. But she had no idea how to help Ainsley understand that without making her mad or hurting her feelings. Maybe if Ainsley saw what she could do with Thunder, as he got better, she'd start to understand and want to learn on her own. Maybe not too, but since Emma wanted to keep teaching Thunder fun skills anyway, she decided that was her "2 birds, 1 stone" plan.

***

"Granny," Emma asked as she slid into the car for their daily Thunder visit, "do you have time to go to the tack store first? It's okay if you don't, no rush, we can go another day."

"I have an hour," Granny said, "and we can use that time however you'd like."

"Tack store please!"

"What are we shopping for, and did you bring your pennies?"

"A halter for Thunder, and yes, I raided my piggy bank." She grinned at Granny. "Okay I don't have a piggy bank, but I did have a little stash of cash left over from my birthday."

"I thought Thunder had a halter? That pretty turquoise one he was wearing when we brought him home?"

"Yeah, but it was a little tight and made marks on his face, plus they left it on him all the time, and I thought it might be better to start with a new one, it might be easier to convince him it was a good thing." Emma shrugged. "Maybe it's silly, but I thought maybe he didn't want that halter on again."

"Makes sense to me," Granny said, "besides, it's your money, you can do whatever silly things you want with it." She stuck her tongue out at Emma and turned towards the local tack store.

Soon they stood in front of the rack with Miniature Horse sized halters on it, and Emma looked in dismay at the limited selection. She was used to a zillion different colour options and combinations when she was looking at full sized horse equipment, and here she saw only plain nylon halters, in one size and three fairly ugly colour options. She wrinkled her nose, just as a voice behind her said, "May I help you?"

Emma turned to the lady. "Are these all the Miniature Horse size halters you have?"

"Hmm," the lady looked unsure. "Let me check, I'm pretty new and we might have more hidden somewhere I don't know about yet, just let me go ask for you."

"Thank you!" Emma smiled at her gratefully and crossed her fingers.

"I don't know," Granny said, "The orange might look quite nice on him."

"Maybe," Emma said doubtfully, "but I don't like it even if it did!"

Granny laughed. "What are you hoping for?"

"Maybe a nice sky blue, to match his eyes?"

"The turquoise did that pretty well I thought," Granny said, then raised her hand before Emma could respond. "I know, I know, the turquoise is out!"

The saleslady reappeared. "I'm afraid those are all the nylon mini sized halters we have, but we do have this as well." She held out a leather halter, with brass fittings, and it was so beautiful that Emma gasped.

She took it in her hands. It was lovely, soft deep brown leather and beautifully sized to fit a small face. "How much?" she asked, looking for a tag, while knowing there was likely no way her little stash of cash would cover it.

"It's $50, but as it's our last one it's on clearance for 50% off."

Emma's eyes widened. "Really?! Yay!"

The saleslady smiled. "I had to knock the dust off of it before I brought it out, I think it must've been waiting for you."

Emma bought Thunder's beautiful new halter, and had just taken her receipt when she spotted the machine that made name plates. "Ooh, Granny, maybe he should have his name on it!"

"Would you put Thunder, or his registered name?"

Emma giggled. "Thunder, definitely." She paused. "Or maybe Magic Thunder."

"Oh," Granny raised her eyebrows. "I didn't realize Thunder was his middle name."

Emma nodded decisively. "Yes, his full name is Magic Thunder Snookums."

The saleslady looked concerned. "I'm not sure that all will fit on a halter plate," she said tentatively.

"It's fine," Emma laughed, "we'll keep thinking about it. Thank you for your help finding this!" She swept up the halter and held it up to admire it as she stepped out into the sunshine and she was still staring at it while Granny pulled out of the parking lot and headed for the farm.

"And it's got the throatlatch snap!" Emma raved, "That means that I should be able to slide it over his ears and put it on him one handed even, before I get the sling off!"

"Once the doctor says you can," Granny amended.

"Once the doctor says I can," Emma agreed.

At the farm, Emma was excited all over again by a pile of colourful plastic poles stacked near her chair and cookie bin next to Thunder's paddock. As they got out of the car Ruby came out of the barn, a wooden jump standard in each hand.

"They're so cute!" Emma squealed in delight, "Perfect jump standards but Thunder sized!"

"They haven't seen much use in probably fifteen years," Ruby said, "not since Sissy moved on to the big horses full time, really, as I'm too old for the running involved. It'll be a real treat to see them enjoyed again, and maybe when you get that shoulder healed up you'll be willing to take a few of my old folks over them again too, they'd love it."

"Oh, I'd love to!" Emma held out the new halter to show her. "Look what we found for Thunder!"

Ruby set down the jump standards to take the halter from her and look at it closely. "Did you get that here in town?" She sounded incredulous.

"Yes! They said it was the last one they had."

"It's beautiful, a good leather halter is so hard to find for these little guys, what a lucky find!" Ruby handed it back to Emma. "Have you shown it to his highness yet?"

"No, but I will, just let me get some cookies!" Emma hurried over and fell to her knees at the bin, filling her pockets, picked up the target in case she needed it, and then went over to the fence and called, "Thunder, I brought you a present, can you come touch?"

Thunder had been at the far end of the paddock nosing around at the ground, but at her call he threw his head up and even gave a small nicker before he trotted across the pen to her. "Good boy," Emma crooned at him, feeding him a treat, then called back, "Did you hear him? He was talking to me!"

"Yes, we heard!" Granny said, "I think I got it on camera, hope you can hear it on the video, so cute!"

Emma held out the halter, and Thunder leaned back, as he always did with new things, but Emma remembered the broom handle and said, "Thunder, can you touch?" treating the halter just like she would've the target. He blinked at her for a moment, but she waited another breath and then he poked his nose out and touched the nearest strap of the halter. Emma clicked her tongue the second that his nose got near it, and fed him. "What a brave boy."

She offered it again, and again, holding it in a different way each time, and he became more and more comfortable. Emma wished she had two hands, then she might be able to hold it with one hand and offer the treat with the other, to see if he would put his head through part of it to get the treat, but really, this was probably good enough for a first introduction.

Quit when it's going well, she thought, and pulled the halter back and rubbed his forehead under his forelock, which he seemed to enjoy more every day.

"How much time is left Granny?" Emma asked, thinking it must be nearly up but really hoping that there was enough time to play a little bit with the jumps.

"Twenty minutes or so."

Emma looked thoughtful. "Do you think it would be against the rules if I went into the pen with him just to set up a jump?"

Ruby grinned. "I'll come with you and protect you from the wild beast if needed," she said, "though I'd bet good money you're as safe in there with him as you are out here, that horse thinks a lot of you, I think he'll be careful of you."

"I'll help too," Granny said, "not to protect you, but to carry stuff because I have two arms."

Emma made a face at her, then grinned.

It felt like quite the momentous occasion when the three of them paraded into the paddock, Granny with two poles and Ruby and Emma each carrying a jump standard. Emma also had her target tucked into her sling, "Just in case," she'd said, but secretly she was hoping she'd get a chance to sneak in a little interaction with Thunder without a fence between them, just to see what he thought of that, if he would trust her without the safety of protective contact.

When the procession started in the gate, Thunder trotted away and stood in the far corner, watching curiously, but standing still, not running around freaking out, which Emma thought was pretty good, considering that if she was a horse and saw three people walking in carrying weird stuff she might've spooked too.

"Where are we headed?" Granny turned around to ask the question, while Ruby secured the gate behind them.

"Over where the broom was yesterday, I think," Emma said, "so that it's nice and flat both for me on the outside and him on the inside."

Emma and Ruby set the jump standards down, one right against the fence, so that Thunder could go along the fence and jump the jump just as he had the broom handle.

Hopefully.

Granny and Ruby set the poles in the two lowest cups on the jump, so the height was higher than the broom had been, but still quite low so that it would be easy for a rookie jumper.

Well, a rookie at jumping "formal" jumps, Emma thought, remembering him jumping the chain link fence.

She looked over to see Thunder had come closer to investigate what was going on. As Ruby and Granny stood back to admire their handiwork on jump set up, Emma spoke up before they could notice what she was doing.

Holding out the target she said, "Thunder can you come touch?" the same as she had so many times from the other side of the fence, and then there was a moment of absolute silence, as everyone froze to see what would happen. Thunder blinked a couple times, and then trotted over, same as always, to put his nose on the familiar blue micro fibre. Emma clicked and fed him a treat, and it felt exactly the same as it had from the other side of the fence, and yet, entirely – monumentally – different too.

"Can you come see this new jump?" Emma walked towards the jump, and he walked along with her, in step just like he always was when she was on the other side of the fence. Ruby and Granny faded back as Emma and Thunder approached, not wanting to overwhelm him, and as per usual when she showed him something new, when he saw the jump he blew loud breaths of air through his nostrils and backed away.

But Emma knew just what to do, because she'd spent the last week getting to know him. She walked over and put her hand on the jump standard. "Thunder, can you touch this?" He was still backing away from it when she spoke, and like she'd flipped a switch he walked forward instead, and touched the standard right next to her hand and she clicked and fed him. She didn't even ask him to touch it again, but he stepped forward and ran his nose along the top jump rail, making it rattle in its cups. Worried he might spook at the sound, Emma quickly clicked and fed him another treat.

Emma avoided looking at her Granny, in case she got a "cease and desist" look from her that she wouldn't be able to ignore, and walked some distance from the jump, gave Thunder, who had walked along with her like she was leading him, another treat, and when he was finished chewing it said, "Let's go!" and jogged towards the jump, because she figured if she was breaking the fence rules she might as well break the running rules too.

She knew it might not work, and half expected Thunder to stop or duck around the jump, and despite what her granny might think, she was being very cautious and aware that he might duck her way to avoid it.

But even while she was ready with contingencies, ready for it not to be successful, she threw all her hopes over the jump, and Thunder went with them, soaring over and then instead of the buck and head tossing he'd done previously to celebrate a fun jump, he trotted in a big circle, floating with his white tail flagging behind him and Emma clicked her tongue, trying to tell him that she loved it, and he trotted right up to her for his treat.

"That's enough, young lady," Her Granny's voice was firm, but also with a hint of laughter. "You'll be pleased to know I got it on video. But you have to tell your mother what you did. When I'm not there."

Emma rubbed Thunder's head, savouring her final few moments with him without the barrier, and celebrating the fact that he was her friend inside the fence too. She thought there was a pretty good chance that he could've reverted to running away crazy when she was on the same side of the fence as he was, and had steeled herself not to be disappointed if he had, since it had only been a week, and he really didn't know her all that well yet.

But, he had trusted her.

It felt a bit like a miracle, and as she gave him a handful of treats on the ground and they headed out, Emma looked fondly at the now grubby blue duster. Who would have ever guessed that such a strange tool would be the difference between a scared and wild horse, and an engaged one who learned so fast she couldn't even believe it.

"Is the jump okay in here?" Emma asked.

Ruby nodded. "He can't hurt it, and I don't think it can hurt him, might as well stay there for now and then it's ready for you to play again tomorrow."

They filed out and Ruby carefully snapped the chain to secure the gate behind them. Thunder had come a long way, but none of them wanted to take any chances on him going on another wild adventure. Emma wondered if he'd come when she called him to touch the target the same way if he was out in the world running wild as he had been the first time she'd seen him.

She thought he probably would, but she definitely didn't want to find out.

"It's amazing," she said, as she stowed away her target and put the lid back on the bin, "every day I think it can't get better, and every day it does. I've never had this much fun with a horse before."

On the way home, she mulled that over some more. It WAS the most fun she'd had with a horse. She'd thought she was having fun riding and competing, but there was none of the joy she felt teaching Thunder to jump. It was hard work, and satisfying, and there were moments of exhilaration, but it was ... different, and Emma was trying to figure out the root of the difference.

Maybe it was the lack of competitive component? But she didn't think that was all it was. Even in competitions, while she liked to win, it was always her main focus to do better than they had last time. When the accident had happened, she'd wanted to win, but winning was foremost on her mind because it was the jump off and the win would've meant that she'd gotten the clear round.

She closed her eyes, and thought about how she felt riding Thor over a jump. It was hard work. She felt like she was fighting him every step of the way, making sure he actually went over the jump instead of stopping or ducking around it. She worked so hard to physically put him over the jump, and when she'd failed they'd both gotten hurt.

With Thunder, it felt like they were playing together, trying something new to see if they could do it.

Emma's eyes flew open. That was it, that was why it was more fun: because it felt like she was on the same team as her horse, instead of constantly fighting against him.

Why did she feel like that? Why hadn't she been on the same team as Thor?

She kept thinking about it long after Granny had dropped her at home. Instead of watching more clicker trainers on YouTube or turning on the tv, Emma just wrapped herself in a blanket in the recliner and thought.

She remembered the first time she'd ridden Thor, and when he'd stopped suddenly to look at something, Ainsley had her kick him until he went forward, because she hadn't told him to stop.

She remembered being in a dressage clinic on Chico, with a former Olympic rider, and when Chico struggled to keep his head down in a balanced frame, the clinician had her use draw reins to give her the power to hold it down.

She remembered her very first official riding lesson, at a barn with a group of adorable ponies not much bigger than

Thunder, when the kindly instructor had told her, "You have to make the pony do what you want."

It wasn't the treats that were the biggest difference, although that was the obvious change.

It was giving the horse a choice and an option to walk away if they felt they needed to.

It was having a clear way to tell them when they got the right answer, instead of always just trying to discourage the wrong answer.

It was working together, instead of fighting against them.

That was why jumping Thunder was more fun, and Emma was convinced it would still be fun if they were working towards the biggest competition, because if they struggled they would figure it out together, working on the same team, instead of her trying to force him into something he didn't understand or wasn't comfortable with.

She was still sitting there, lost in thought, when her mom got home from work.

"Em?" Mom turned on the light in the living room, "Are you napping?"

Emma stretched her good arm over her head, "Just thinking."

"Everything okay?" Mom sat down on the couch, settling into her favourite corner.

"Yes, fine," Emma said, "Just thinking about horse training, and trying to figure out why it's so much more fun and feels so much easier working with Thunder than anything I've ever done with horses before."

"Hmm," Mom raised an eyebrow, "That does sound like deep thoughts. Is it because he's so little? Or because of the treats?"

"No, I think it's because he had gotten so bad about being dragged around that we couldn't do that, so had to find another way to explain things to him. And now we're on the same team, instead of always trying to make him do what I want."

"Oh!" Mom opened her eyes wide. "That sounds like quite an epiphany." She thought for a moment. "You're right you know. I only know horse stuff from watching you do it, but I swear you've been told from the first time you were on a horse how you have to make them do what you want, you have to be in charge. I thought that first day, 'why can't she just ask nicely?' but then it seemed to just be the way it was, and I never thought to ask again." She frowned. "Maybe it's because Thunder is small? I mean, I know Thunder could hurt someone too, maybe you'll have to, you know, show him who's boss once you don't have a fence between you?"

"Well ..." Emma flushed, and got her phone out, "Don't be mad, we were just in the pen to set up a proper jump for him and ...." She let her voice trail off and handed her mom the phone, with the video that Granny had sent her ready to play.

"What did you do now?" Her mom reached over to take the phone. Her voice sounded resigned, though she glared over the top of the phone at Emma for a few seconds.

"Just watch the video!" Emma said, and touched the play button.

The video started on Emma, holding out the target and saying, "Thunder, can you touch?" and her mom rolled her eyes when she realized Emma was in the paddock with him, but then widened them in surprise as Thunder came trotting into view, touched his target, got his treat, and then walked off quietly at her side, just like she was leading him, but there was no halter or lead rope connecting them.

"Is this the same horse?!" Her mom asked incredulously. "The one that dragged that Jake boy around and reared and struck and stomped on his foot?"

"Yes, only now no one is trying to force him to do anything." Emma said. "Now we're on the same team."

Her mom watched as Thunder checked out the new jump. "Oh, he's scared of it! Oh! Wow! You asked him to touch it, and then he decided it wasn't scary anymore, that's amazing!" Next she watched as they lined up to the jump. "Emma, you're running and you're not supposed to run OR be in the pen with him – oh my goodness, look at him jump! Oh, he's so happy look at him go with that tail again! Oh wait, he's coming right back to you!" She looked up at Emma. "Wow."

"I know!" Emma said, "And I can't see how any of that has anything to do with his size."

"Well, I would hope that if he was as big as Thor you might've actually listened to the doctor and your mother." Mom shook a finger in her direction.

Emma waved her hand dismissively, then reconsidered. "I might not be able to run fast enough for Thor," she said, tipping her head as she thought, "though once Thunder got the idea with the broomstick he just ran off ahead of me, so maybe that's how it could work with Thor too. Or maybe two people? So he could go from one to the other?"

"No!" Her mom said emphatically.

"I mean when I'm all healed up," Emma said, placatingly. "Not now, Thor isn't allowed to jump for at least six months anyway."

"Thank goodness for that," her mom said, lifting the phone again, "I want to watch it one more time."

Emma would've liked to send the video to Ainsley, but she thought it might not be well received since she'd only just the day before refused to let Ainsley go in the paddock with him, and then there Emma was in the pen. So instead, she took a screenshot of Thunder sailing over the jump, and cropped it just to the jump, so there was no sign of herself in the photo at all, and sent that, because it felt too weird not to send her anything.

And then she made it her profile photo, because Thunder was so handsome and his form was perfect.

She immediately started getting comments on the photo from her friends, things like, "I wish he was big enough to ride, he could show in the International Ring at Spruce Meadows!" and "Sooooo cute!" and "Look at him go!"

But it wasn't long before she did get a text back from Ainsley, and she crossed her fingers and opened it.

Ainsley hadn't commented on the photo Emma had sent at all, but instead just sent a photo of Thor in return, all four of his legs bandaged (Emma worried about that and wondered why) and in his stall, licking the treat that she and her mom had picked out for him. That was nice to see, Emma thought, but she would've felt better if Ainsley had sent at least an emoji as well.

She wished she could talk to Ainsley about the different approach to training. She wondered if she could make her understand that she didn't think it was the treats that were the key to the difference she'd noticed, but instead the difference between working with your horse, and working against them. What would Ainsley say if Emma asked her if she thought she was on the same team as her horse? What would Emma have said, before she got hurt, before she met Thunder?

Though she tried to think back, Emma wasn't sure what she would've said. She would've *wanted* to say that she and Thor were a team, but that wasn't ever really how she'd felt. They weren't working together, she was always working so hard to get him to do what she wanted. Had she ever even thought about what Thor wanted?

She loved Thor though, she really did. She loved how he ate peppermints, and she loved soaring through the air, propelled by his strength and talent.

Emma wondered if she'd ever have a chance to really make friends with him. He had a long recovery ahead of him too, and it would be the perfect time, if Ainsley would let her try to teach him a target. But she was so against it, she thought it was silly, and would make him mouthy – or maybe 'mouthier' might be more accurate. Emma remembered how Ainsley had stood between her and Thor when he knew she had peppermints.

He was so excited about peppermints. What was it that the positive reinforcement trainer had called that? She scrambled for her notebook. Ah, there it was, 'high value treats' – that were super exciting for the horse, and sometimes they couldn't focus and learn. And then 'low value treats' would be better for teaching the target. There was a big bin of alfalfa pellets in the feed room, and she would often give Thor some to munch on before or after she rode him, so those would be fine – he liked them, but they didn't make him lose his mind with excitement. She could save the peppermint til after the training session, and she could leave him happily sucking on one when she left.

That is, if there was any way that she could convince Ainsley to let her work with him.

It would be safe, that couldn't be an argument. He'd be in the stall, and she'd work with him over the stall gate, just like they'd worked with the Arabian mare, Rosebud, at the clinic, only this time the protective contact would primarily be for her safety instead of the horse's confidence.

If she could teach Thor to touch a target, and if he got as comfortable with it as Thunder had, then his handwalking might go much more smoothly. Maybe he wouldn't need the chain through his mouth anymore. Maybe he wouldn't need the chain at all anymore. Heck, maybe not even the halter, based on what she was already doing with Thunder!

Okay, maybe that was a bit of a daydream, but even if, when Jamie was walking him, she could get him to focus back to the target, then maybe he wouldn't rear and be so crazy, and it would be safer for them both. Because that leaping around couldn't be good for Thor's healing leg.

Emma made a decision.

It was scary to think of asking Ainsley about it, when she'd made it so clear she thought the whole training approach was silly or even dangerous, but even if it gave Thor something fun to do during his stall rest then it would be worth it. She wouldn't mention the training benefits, and getting him to lead using the target, she'd just focus on something fun to keep him busy during stall rest, and keep her busy during her recovery too.

She picked up her phone and replied to the text from Ainsley with the photo of Thor.

"I miss him so much! Do you think it would be okay if I came and taught him to touch a target, like Thunder? I can work over the stall door, so it would be safe, and use alfalfa pellets instead of peppermints, so he doesn't get too excited. Then I'll get to spend some time with him, and he'll have something fun to do on his stall rest. I hope he's healing well, let me know! ♥"

She crossed her fingers, and her eyes, and pushed send before she could chicken out.

Then she told herself that the worst that could happen was that Ainsley said no.

Chapter 17

By morning, when she still hadn't heard back from Ainsley, Emma decided that maybe no wasn't the worst that could happen.

Don't be silly, Emma thought to herself, as she brushed her teeth. *She's just busy, that's all, she'll text sometime today.*

She found herself staring at her phone over her breakfast, as it sat silently on the table next to her plate, and she was so focused that her mom noticed.

"You expecting that phone to do a dance or something?"

Emma groaned and laid her head on the table next to the phone. "I'm waiting for a text back from Ainsley and I'm afraid she's mad and ghosting me." She told her mom the whole story.

"I think that's a great idea, and it sounds like you did a great job of asking without pushing any of her buttons." Her mom had listened seriously, not dismissing her thoughts about Thor or her worries about Ainsley. "I'm sure she's just busy." Her mom leaned forward and moved the phone, setting it under her empty plate. "A watched phone never buzzes," she explained with a wink.

As though on cue, and magnified by the plate rattling on top of it, the phone buzzed and they both jumped, then giggled.

The plate hit the table with a clatter as Emma snatched the phone.

But the text wasn't from Ainsley, it was from Maria, her best barn friend. "Did you hear about Ainsley?" and Emma's stomach dropped.

"What does THAT mean?" she said, showing it to her mom.

"Ask her," her mom said, and lines of concern creased her forehead.

Emma texted back, "No, is everything okay?" and then stared at the phone, willing it to buzz. When it did she snatched it up so fast that she nearly dropped it.

"She was handwalking Thor last night, and he went crazy, reared and caught her arm when he came down. We all heard the crack of her bone ◈ but she managed to hold him with her other hand til Jamie ran over to take him, so Thor didn't get away and hurt his leg again."

They only had time to read the text and look at each other in shock before the phone buzzed again and Emma and her mom looked down in unison to read the next text from Maria.

"The ambulance came and took her to the hospital. Last I heard before I left the barn last night she was going to have to have surgery to put in a plate. Was hoping you'd heard something this morning. Let me know if you do!"

Emma scrambled to text back. "Haven't heard anything, thanks for letting me know!"

Emma's mom was always good in a crisis, and she took over. "You text Ainsley, tell her we're thinking of her and let her know we're here to help, anything she needs." She reached for her own phone. "I'm going to call Jamie at the barn." She glanced at the clock. "While I get ready for work." She put the phone to her ear and Emma heard her say, "Jamie, we just heard!" as she walked out of the room.

Wishing she could eavesdrop, but knowing that her mom would give her all the details as soon as she got off the phone, Emma did as instructed and opened the text conversation with Ainsley.

"We just heard about your arm. I hope things are going okay. We're thinking of you, and if you need ANYTHING let us know. I'll get Granny to drive me over to bring you McNuggets if you want! The food is gross at the hospital, I know, I was just there. Hope you get to come home soon. Seriously, if you need ANYTHING text me."

Emma thought that was probably way too rambling, but Ainsley was used to her being a chatterbox and hit send.

Then she texted Granny. She would want to know too, and sure enough Granny texted back right away.

"Oh no! Poor Ainsley! Tell her that we'll smuggle her in McNuggets, just give us the word! Keep me updated!"

Emma grinned. She and Granny were always on the same page when it came to McNuggets.

She was still looking at it when another message popped up, this one from Ainsley herself.

"Thanks Em, I appreciate it! I'm okay, but still waiting for surgery so McNuggets aren't allowed yet. Hopefully this afternoon I'll be all patched up with a steel plate to make me bionic! I will text this evening."

Emma was in the middle of texting her best wishes for crossed fingers for a smooth surgery, when her mom walked back into the room, saying, "Jamie says they think Ainsley's surgery ..." and Emma interrupted to finish her sentence, "is this afternoon!" She showed her mom the text.

"I hope there isn't too much damage, and they can fix her up this afternoon." Mom looked at the clock again. "I'm going to be late if I don't go right now." She grabbed her purse and headed to the door, then turned around and kissed Emma's forehead. "You text me if you hear anything okay?" She opened the door then turned back again, "Oh, and text Granny, she'll want to know!"

"I already did!" Emma called and her mom hollered back "Good girl, love you!" as the door closed behind her.

Emma sank down into the chair she'd been sitting in eating breakfast just a few minutes ago, and felt kind of numb. What was she supposed to do now?

If she hadn't been laid up herself, she could've gone to the barn and helped with chores at least, cleaned some stalls and then she'd feel like she was helping.

Of course, if she wasn't laid up, she'd be at school today, like Maria.

Maria!

Emma picked up her phone yet again to tell Maria that Ainsley was having surgery this afternoon, and then tossed it back onto the table.

Now what?

Her phone buzzed and she looked down, expecting a text from Maria, but it was Granny.

"Free at 11 for a Thunder visit?"

She texted back, "YES PLEASE," and looked at the clock and sighed. Only two and a half hours to kill, but at least she had something to look forward to other than wondering how Ainsley was doing. And Thor. It broke her heart that he was so crazy from his stall rest that he'd hurt Ainsley. It was so lucky she'd been able to hold him, that was amazing, doing whatever it took to keep him safe. That's why it was so strange to Emma that she didn't want to learn about training with positive re-inforcement. Ainsley would do anything for her horses, even hanging onto Thor with a badly broken arm. If it was better for the horses, why wouldn't she want to learn everything she could about it?

Suddenly, Emma knew what she was going to do this morn-ing. She looked at her phone, and decided this research project needed the computer, and headed to her room, and the laptop on her desk. Ignoring the stack of school work that was wait-ing until her concussion healed, and the fact that she probably could've been doing homework for days now, she turned on the laptop, opened a new browser window and typed into the search bar.

Positive reinforcement stall rest

This time, she'd used the right terms, and got a whole list of articles and videos and ideas, and she ran back to the living room to fetch her trusty notebook and started making notes.

When she'd exhausted that topic, and had a zillion ideas written down, some that would work for Thor, some that really wouldn't but were still interesting enough she wanted to share them with Ainsley, she started a new search.

Positive reinforcement show jumping

Emma was still reading and scribbling and even printing when she heard Granny call, "Em, where are you?" and she closed the laptop with a bang, grabbed her notebook and scrambled out of the room.

"Here, Granny, sorry I got all wrapped up in some research and didn't realize it was time already!"

"Research? Are you back working on school work?"

Emma made a face. "No," she said, "I mean, I probably should be, but, no. Just more positive reinforcement stuff. Did you know that there's a grand prix show jumper that wouldn't go over water jumps, so they clicker trained him to do it, and now he jumps them every time?"

"I definitely did not know that," said Granny, "And I'm not quite sure of the significance either, but it does seem like something you should share with poor Ainsley when she's feeling better." She winked at Emma. "Maybe if you just bombard her with links to articles and videos while she's laid up in bed she'll have to come around."

That made Emma laugh. "I'll see what I can come up with." She stepped into her boots, scooped Thunder's fancy new halter off the hook in the entryway, and locked the door behind them.

***

Ruby was shocked to hear about Ainsley's injury, and promptly pulled her phone out to send her a text. She squinted at the phone. "Oh, I don't have my glasses on." She handed her phone to Emma. "Can you send a text to Ainsley? She's in there under Sissy." She dictated the message, and when Emma handed the phone back, message sending her love sent, she popped it in her pocket. "That horse is dangerous, isn't he? He's taken out two of you now!"

"No!" Emma was shocked at the suggestion at first, then shrugged. "I guess I can see why you'd think that though, he did put two of us in the hospital within just a few weeks, didn't he?"

"The evidence is against him." Ruby's voice was dry.

"But he isn't dangerous, not really. I think," Emma hesitated, "I think I got hurt because he was scared, or just couldn't do what I was asking, and I didn't listen to him. I didn't know how to listen to horses, and I still wouldn't have known, but Thunder taught me. And Thor got hurt too, because I didn't listen to all the times he blew a scared dragon breath at a jump, or stopped, or spooked. I just kept forcing him over them, and this time he couldn't do it, and he fell." She spoke in a monotone, looking off into the distance. "And Ainsley got hurt because he already didn't really know how to lead, we always just used a chain and tried to muscle him around, and now he's all crazy from not getting any exercise like a horse is supposed to, and so they had to use a chain through his mouth." Emma's face crumpled, but she didn't cry. "No wonder he felt he had to fight back."

Ruby reached out and squeezed her good shoulder. "You have a good heart, Emma."

Granny was quiet for a moment, then she asked Emma a question, watching her curiously as she answered. "Do you think that the same thing you did with Thunder would help him? The duster and the cookies and staying outside the fence?"

Emma gave a wan smile. "I think it would be worth a try."

"So do I," Granny said, "It's only been a week and that one," she nodded at Thunder, "has gone from running away and rearing and being a wild thing to following you like a puppy dog."

Ruby looked thoughtful. "Does Sissy know what you've been doing here?"

Emma tipped her head back and forth in an uncertain gesture. "Sorta. She didn't like the idea of using treats for training. She said it was silly, and would make him dangerous. Then she got mad when I told her I didn't want her to corner him and get a halter on him. So, I didn't share that much with her after that, I didn't want to make her mad again."

Ruby raised her eyebrows, and Emma realized she hadn't had any idea about the conflict between Emma and Ainsley over Thunder's training. "Well," Ruby said at last, "I think it's high time she opened her mind a little and saw what you've been doing here. Change isn't easy for anyone, least of all an old bat like me, but even I can see the good you've done, and the potential uses for the tools you've learned."

"She did say maybe we could smuggle her in some McNuggets after her surgery," Emma said, "I'll try again then. I'll tell her all about Thunder, and the clinic, and show her all the videos we've taken, and I've been taking notes and doing research." She ran over and grabbed her notebook out of the car, flipping it open with help from her slinged hand. "A whole bunch of ideas to use positive reinforcement to help horses who have to be on stall rest." She turned pages with a bit of difficulty. "And here, I was just working on examples of how people have used positive reinforcement to help their show jumpers, and how to do it." She fumbled the notebook, and Ruby caught it before it hit the ground, reading thoughtfully.

"You've done a ton of work here," Ruby said, "and neatly organized too."

Emma flushed. "Mom would say, 'why can't you put that much effort into your school work.'"

Ruby laughed. "Moms always say that, I know, I am one. But," she leaned forward conspiratorially, "no one said you couldn't make all your school projects something to do with horses." She handed the notebook back. "I think if you throw all that at Sissy she's going to have to start changing her thinking. Be patient with her though, you know how hard it is to think that you weren't listening to Thor, well Sissy's got fifteen or twenty years of horse experience, and it's not easy to think that you could've done better by the horses in your care. She's always done her best."

"Of course she has!" Emma was a bit shocked. "No one ever cared more about the horses than Ainsley! Even when Thor broke her arm she didn't let him go, because she didn't want him to get hurt."

Ruby looked a bit like she wanted to cry, and Emma was sorry she'd brought it up, but all Ruby said was, "That's our Sissy, she was always a tough one." She clapped her hands together. "So, what are you planning for his highness today?"

Emma held up the halter. "I'd like to see if he'd put his nose in the halter," she said, "But I might need to borrow another set of hands. Do you think he'd take a treat from one of you?"

Ruby held her hand up to her mouth like she was telling a secret. "I may or may not give him one every morning and night when I throw him his hay." She grinned. "He asks so nicely I can't say no!"

"Oh yay, that's great!" Emma said, "Let's give it a try. I'll hold the halter and you hold the target and the cookie."

Granny held up her phone. "And I'll be videographer. For posterity."

They went to the gate, because it was made of horizontal pipe and had wider spaces to work through than the wire mesh fence. Thunder trotted over even before Emma called him, and she had to scramble to go get him a treat to reward that good choice. She talked to him while Ruby moved the tub close for easy access and took a handful to get herself started. "Now Thunder," she said, opening the buckle on the halter crownpiece to open it as big as it would go, and then unsnapping the throatlatch. "I'm going to hold up this halter like this," she held it by the crownpiece to demonstrate, and was pleased to see it was sturdy enough that the noseband held a nice open space. "And you are going to have to reach through to touch your target. First just through the main part of the halter I think," she looked at Ruby to see if she agreed.

"Sounds logical to me."

"And if it goes well maybe under the crownpiece and nose through the noseband even." She fiddled one more time with the adjustment. "I've got it as big as it goes, so it shouldn't even touch your ears, and I won't let go of it, so it won't stay on your head today, we're just practicing pop your head in and get a yummy treat and pop your head out again."

Granny spoke up from the background. "You'd swear he's listening to you." And it was true, Thunder was looking at her with ears pricked and eyes bright, following her every move as she gestured with the halter.

"Well let's see what he says," Ruby said, and Emma put the halter into the pen, dangling from her good hand. Ruby held the target right inside the halter at first, so Thunder barely had to put his nose past the strap of the crownpiece to touch it, and though Emma could feel his breath as he huffed as he passed her hand, he didn't seem to hesitate. She clicked her tongue just as he touched it. He didn't linger, and pulled back quickly, and Ruby handed him a treat. It seemed like a great first step and Emma and Ruby grinned at each other.

Over the next few minutes they made slow but steady progress. They discussed it, and didn't want to make it harder every time, so sometimes Ruby held the target quite far past the halter, so he had to be brave and go through right to his eyes, or sometimes she put the target closer, so he didn't actually have to reach through at all. He seemed to get more and more interested, as he figured out the game.

"I think that's quite good for today," said Emma, "he's gotten so comfortable with sticking his nose under the strap, right up til nearly his whole head is through."

"Let's try one through the noseband," suggested Ruby, "after all, if he says no I'll just readjust and offer it where he is comfortable."

Emma agreed, thinking again how much easier it was when she knew Thunder had a way to tell her when he wasn't comfortable.

Thunder seemed to hesitate for a millisecond when he saw the target in a new place, but before Emma could even think that they'd made a mistake, he poked his head under the crownpiece and dropped his nose through the loop of the noseband to touch the target as calmly as any other time, and then quietly ducked out of it again. Emma had forgotten to click she'd been so surprised, but she hoped that her and Ruby's chorus of, "Good boy!" followed by handfuls of treats had the same effect.

"I know I'm not a horse person like you two are, "Granny said, lowering her phone as they stepped away from the gate, "but it seems to me a little unusual to have a horse who puts his own halter on!"

Emma laughed delightedly. "It was pretty cool! Imagine how good he'll be tomorrow, because he totally seems to think things over and be even better the next day."

"I'm sure he does," Ruby said, "Mine always seemed to do that, and they weren't learning to think and problem solve quite like this guy is." She rubbed her chin. "Would you mind if I borrowed this duster of yours? I'd like to start playing with mine a bit, see if I can teach old horses new tricks."

"Of course!" said Emma, reaching to take the offered target, "Do we have time for a jump or two, Granny?"

Granny raised her phone. "You betcha, videographer standing by!"

***

It was after supper before Emma got another text from Ainsley.

"Out of surgery. Doc says all went well. Got the good drugs. Turning off my phone and going to sleep, will chat tomorrow about those McNuggets. Send photos of Thunder being adorable to cheer me up when I wake up."

Emma breathed a sigh of relief that all had gone well, and sent the video Granny had taken of Thunder jumping today, and then, after a moment of hesitation, sent the haltering video too.

If she was going to tell her all about it next time she saw her, she might as well see it with her own eyes. For better or for worse.

Chapter 18

"Are you sure you don't want me to come with you?" Granny leaned over from the drivers seat, watching as Emma tucked a McDonalds bag, a bouquet of flowers, her notebook and her phone into a shoulder bag so she could carry it all one handed.

"I know my way around the hospital pretty well after I spent all those days here," Emma spoke cheerfully, trying to hide any nervousness about the visit, though Granny's concern meant she wasn't being completely successful. "And Ainsley's even in the same ward that I was, maybe it's the 'horse injury ward'." Emma giggled at that idea. "I'll text you if I need to be picked up sooner, otherwise I'll meet you back here in an hour."

"All right, lovey, call if you need anything, and have a good visit! Tell Ainsley that your mom and I are thinking of her." Granny waved as she drove off, and Emma turned and walked through the big doors into the main entrance of the hospital.

She walked confidently towards the elevators, and waited her turn, then punched the button for the fourth floor. She walked out and headed right, glad for the silver lining of knowing just where to go.

Emma approached the nursing station with a smile and asked the nurse on duty which room Ainsley was in, signed in as a visitor, and followed the nurse's directions to find the right room number. The room door stood open, and Ainsley walked in tentatively. There was a very old lady in the first bed she saw, fast asleep and looking cozy wrapped up in blankets, and Emma hurried through to the bed on the far side of the curtain, and there was Ainsley, sitting up in bed, her arm in a huge brace and bandage propped up on pillows. She was looking at her phone, her face serious.

"Aw," Emma said, "I was hoping you'd have a sling like me so we could match!"

Ainsley looked up at her words and her face lit up. "Emma!" She looked down at her arm and grinned, "Soon, I guess, they tell me that I'll get a sling tomorrow, and then maybe I can go home."

"So soon, that's great! I had to stay much longer." Emma hoisted her bag onto the foot of the bed, ducked out of the shoulder strap and started rummaging inside.

"That's because you had head trauma too," Ainsley sat up, looking eager to see what Emma was rummaging for. "This is just a flesh wound."

"I'm pretty sure that flesh wounds don't require steel plates to fix them," Emma said, emerging with the McDonalds bag and handing it to Ainsley, who snatched it eagerly.

"Oh, you are an absolute angel!" Ainsley worked at getting her McNuggets out and set on the rolling table next to her bed, then got out the sauce and looked at it for a moment, before she put it up to her mouth and pulled the lid off with her teeth.

Emma giggled watching her. "See, you're getting the hang of this one handed thing already!"

"Ugh," Ainsley said, "At least it's your left arm and my right, if we work together we'll have a complete set." She dipped a nugget and took a bite. "You remembered, barbeque sauce, not sweet and sour!"

"Of course I remembered," Emma said, "I take McNuggets very seriously, even if you're wrong about your sauce choices."

Ainsley made a show of how much she enjoyed the next bite of the 'wrong' sauce. "Oh!" she said, still chewing the nugget. "I had the same surgeon that you did! He says he's going to have to put Thor on the payroll, he's bringing him so much business." It was supposed to be a joke, but neither of them laughed. "I told him we were going to find a way to make sure it didn't happen again."

It seemed like the perfect time to bring up Emma's ideas for Thor, but she thought it was better to let Ainsley at least finish eating before she risked making her mad, so instead she got the flowers out of the bag and started removing the protective wrapping paper. "These are from me and Mom and Granny." She looked around the room and spotted a sink. "I had to dump the water out to stash them in the bag, but they don't seem too worse for wear," she said over her shoulder as she filled the vase at the sink, then set them on the window sill, next to two other bouquets.

"One from Jamie and the girls at the barn, the other my mum brought this morning." Ainsley said seeing Emma look at them, "Yours are lovely, and I know it wasn't easy to get them up here with one arm, so extra thanks for that, they look beautiful!"

Emma found a chair in the corner and dragged it closer to the bed. She didn't know what to say next, so she thought for a moment. What did she *most* want to say to Ainsley? Then it came to her.

"I think it was amazing you were still able to hold onto Thor," she said in a rush, "He didn't get hurt again because of you. You kept him safe." Emma was a bit surprised to find tears springing to her eyes.

"Emma." Ainsley's voice was serious. "It really, and truly, wasn't your fault that Thor got hurt. I feel like you still don't believe that."

"I don't." Emma said simply, sniffing as she tried to stop the tears.

"Why do you say that?" Ainsley set down her nugget and reached her good arm across to squeeze Emma's knee. "Because I was there, I can't see anything you could've done in the moment."

"He was trying to tell me he wasn't comfortable. I don't know if he was scared, or if he just couldn't do it, but he said no, and I ignored it, like I always do, and made him do it anyway. This time, he couldn't do it anyway, and we both got hurt." Emma looked at her lap. "Because I didn't listen to him."

Ainsley was quiet for a long time and when she spoke her voice was soft. "You did exactly what I taught you to do."

Emma looked up sharply to see Ainsley looking as hunched and sad as she had felt when she'd realized there was a better way and thought back to all the things she'd done in the past. "It was what everyone had taught me. Every clinic I went to. Even my very first lesson on Mrs. Jones' ponies. No one ever said anything to me about listening to the horse when they say no. They all said I had to be the boss." Emma grabbed Ainsley's hand, trying to make her understand that it wasn't her fault either. "You taught me so much about horses. You taught me that the horse comes first. That's how I was able to listen when Thunder taught me how."

Ainsley managed a weak smile as she squeezed Emma's hand, but there were tears in her eyes too. "Tell me about it," she said, "I'm ready to listen." She let go of Emma's hand and held it up. "I'm not drinking the koolaid yet," she said, "but I want to hear the whole story, from the beginning, and everything you learned at that clinic, and all the decisions you made to make Thunder follow you and jump over jumps and put his own head in a halter."

"Okay, I better get my notebook then," Emma leaped up and stepped to the end of the bed where she'd left her bag, and checked her phone while she was there, "And we better hurry, it's only half an hour until I need to meet Granny."

Ainsley's eyes widened in amazement as she saw the pages of notes that Emma was flipping through in her now worn and dogeared notebook. "Ruby was here first thing this morning, and she warned me that you'd have a whole presentation prepared," she said, "and she made it clear that I better listen to it with an open mind, because, and I quote, 'if an old bat like me can have an open mind and see the good of a new training method, then so can you.'" Ainsley's usual grin was returning to her face, "And she sent me a whole bunch of videos of Thunder, in order, so I could – and again I quote – 'study his progress', so that's what I was doing when you came in." She settled into the pillows at a comfy angle to see the notebook in Emma's hands. "Can you start with the duster? Because I totally don't get that part."

Emma felt like a huge weight had been lifted from her shoulders. She didn't mind the bit of scepticism that Ainsley still had. She knew that Ainsley cared about the horses in her care more than anything, and was sure that she would be able to convince her the value of the things she'd learned, once she understood how much better it was for the horses. But even more than that, she was so grateful to have Ainsley back on her team. It had been too weird not to have her to share every bit of her horse adventures.

With a deep breath, Emma settled in to try and tell Ainsley everything she'd learned about using positive reinforcement to train a horse before Granny came to pick her up.

She failed miserably, but Ainsley seemed very interested in everything she said, asked good questions, and when she had to go took photos of some of the pages of the notebook so she could look some things up and keep learning on her own. "After all," said Ainsley, "what else have I got to do laying here?"

Before Emma left, she gave Ainsley an extremely awkward one arm to one arm hug, that still managed to be very warm and comforting.

"Thank you for listening," Emma said.

"Thank you for trying until I could hear you," Ainsley said.

Chapter 19

Epilogue

Three Weeks Later

"Are you kidding me?" Ainsley said in disbelief, as she watched Emma lead Thunder around his paddock on a loose lead rope snapped onto his gleaming leather halter.

"Open the gate!" Emma called cheerfully, "My sling is off and doctor says as long as I only hold the lead rope in my right hand for another two weeks I'm allowed to, quote," she held up her now free hand in air quotes, "'horse around' again."

Ainsley laughed as she swung the gate wide. She had also been able to ditch her sling, but a lime green cast was still visible at the cuff of her winter coat. "Today's the big day, is it?"

Emma walked out, Thunder at her side, lead draped between them with no pressure from either side of the partnership. She stopped and fed him. "We've practiced leading in the pen, and in the yard with the gate closed, and it's all gone perfectly. The consensus was that if you'd come with me, we could go for a walk down the road. Besides," Emma added, "I was at physio this morning and they put so much tape on my shoulder I think that should hold it together if anything were to happen."

Thunder's ears were up and eyes bright as he walked along at Emma's side. He sniffed the air and whinnied as they walked towards the main gate to the property, but when Emma stopped, so did he, and she gave him a treat for listening so well when he was clearly excited about the outing. "What a good boy you are!"

"He really is," Ainsley said, "Oh, wait, let me get a video of the monumental moment that he walks out in the world as a good boy!" She got her phone out and dropped behind to get a good angle of the moment that he went through the gate and headed down the road. "He's so different! Remember when I led him off the trailer that night? He was good, after he realized he couldn't get away on me, but he wasn't paying attention to anything, just like a little robot shuffling along. Now he's so happy, looking around and bright and practically prancing, but he never tightens that leadrope at all!"

"I was reading about that too," Emma said, "they said it's called 'learned helplessness', when the horse has learned that nothing they do makes any difference anyway, so they just give up and stop trying, just a survival mode."

"Oh," Ainsley said, "That's so sad, I don't know if I want to learn more about that, but sounds like I should. Send me a link when you get home."

A distant rumble warned them that a car was approaching, and they stepped as far off to the side as they could, unable to go down into the ditch because it was deep with snow, but the driver slowed accommodatingly and Thunder just watched it curiously, while Emma fed him treats to reinforce what a good and calm boy he was being. They caught a glimpse of the driver, sneaking a quick photo of the tiny horse with a big grin on her face as she went past.

"I nearly forgot!" Ainsley said as they started walking out again. "I wanted to tell you, I spoke to the positive reinforcement trainer, the one that you learned from at the clinic at Green's barn, and even though she lives a couple hours away, she said she'd do a virtual consult on the best way to approach

Thor, and start using these techniques to help him with his stall rest, and his confidence. It's set up for tomorrow, did you want to come be there with me? You take better notes than I do, and soon you'll be working with Thor as much as anyone, would be good to have you there."

"Of course!" Emma said, "I'm glad it's on the weekend, this having to go back to school every day is putting a huge crimp in my horse time." She made a funny face and winked at Ainsley.

Emma watched Thunder as he stepped out eagerly next to her, his white mane and tail free of tangles and floating around him with every step, bright blue eyes sparkling in the bright sunshine, reflecting the snowy world around them. "He's having so much fun," she said, her heart warming at how happy and brave and just plain beautiful he was.

Another vehicle was coming, and they tucked up to the edge of the snowbank again to leave space. But this time, instead of going slowly past, the rusty old pickup stopped, and Emma looked up from feeding Thunder into a familiar face. "Hi!" she said, at the same time as Ainsley said, "It's Jake, right?"

Jake nodded mutely, staring at Thunder. "Is that the same pony?"

"Yes!" Emma grinned at the pony in question. "I call him Thunder, isn't he beautiful?"

"Why isn't he dragging you around anymore?" Jake sounded suspicious.

"Because Emma taught him that she was on his side, and wouldn't drag him around." Ainsley said proudly, and Emma glowed with happiness at her words.

"But, he broke my toe jumping into the trailer that night," Jake said, sounding a little whiny about it, "and now he's leading like an angel. How did you do it?"

"With an extendable duster from the dollar store and bag of horse treats!" Emma said, grinning at how silly it sounded.

"Fine," Jake said sulkily, "don't tell me." He started to pull away, but Emma stopped him.

"Wait, no, really!" She looked at him earnestly, ducking her head to see in the window better. "I'm not making fun, that's really what I used. If you're interested, I can show you, we should probably head back anyway, if you want to meet us at Cool Waters Miniature Horse Farm." She pointed in the direction of the farm.

"I know where it is," Jake said, "I stack hay for Ruby." He looked at her for a moment, and Emma couldn't read his expression. "I'm on my way to work right now, but maybe one day after school? I'd like to see this sorcery."

"Sure," Emma said in surprise, not really expecting him to be interested. Jake pulled away and she called after him, "Sorry about your toe!"

"He's cute," Ainsley said as they turned back towards the farm. "I think he likes you!" she said, a singsong lilt to her voice.

Emma gave her a shove, grateful for the luxury of her second arm back so she could do so while holding Thunder's lead securely in the other hand, and then ignored the teasing.

The sun was shining, her very own horse Thunder walked at her side, enjoying the walk as much as she was, and she had her friendship with Ainsley back and better than ever.

She couldn't wait to see what they could do together next.

Kendra Gale is the author of the Big Book of Miniature Horses, the must-have primer on all things Miniature Horse, and teaches humans to have more fun with their Miniature Horses through her online classroom and community at Miniature-Horsemanship.com

Ever since her grandparents brought home three Miniature Horses when Kendra was just a toddler, she has dedicated her whole life to learning more about how to better care for and communicate with the very special Miniature Horses in her life. Just like some of the characters in this book, when Kendra first began exploring the use of positive reinforcement, it wasn't easy to let go of the old ways, and admit that there was a better way than the way she'd been doing it for so many years, but she's so grateful she finally made the switch.

Having more fun than ever training her Miniature Horses, Kendra loves to compete in horse agility, Miniature Horse shows, and combined driving, and trick and liberty training is a favourite activity.

If you'd like to learn more about reward based training for Miniature Horses, the Introduction to Positive Reinforcement online course will get you started on the right foot.

This course will introduce you to the concept of positive reinforcement, explaining why it's so powerful – it seems like magic, but it's actually science! – and giving clear instructions for you to begin using this form of communication with your Miniature Horse.

With a step by step learning process, including both teaching and demonstration videos, at the completion of this course both you and your horse will be ready to incorporate this powerful tool into your everyday training, helping you to excel in whatever you'd like to accomplish.

classroom.miniaturehorsemanship.com/reward